Restricted Access

Read all the books in the
**TOM SWIFT INVENTORS'
ACADEMY** series!

The Drone Pursuit
The Sonic Breach
Restricted Access

TOM SWIFT

INVENTORS' ACADEMY

-BOOK 3-

Restricted Access

VICTOR APPLETON

Aladdin
NEW YORK LONDON TORONTO SYDNEY NEW DELHI

ALADDIN

An imprint of Simon & Schuster Children's Publishing Division

1230 Avenue of the Americas, New York, New York 10020

First Aladdin hardcover edition October 2019

Text copyright © 2019 by Victor Appleton

Jacket illustration copyright © 2019 by Kevin Keele

TOM SWIFT, TOM SWIFT INVENTORS' ACADEMY, and related logos are trademarks of Simon & Schuster, Inc.

Also available in an Aladdin paperback edition.

All rights reserved, including the right of reproduction in whole or in part in any form.

ALADDIN and related logo are registered trademarks of Simon & Schuster, Inc.

For information about special discounts for bulk purchases, please contact Simon & Schuster Special Sales at 1-866-506-1949 or business@simonandschuster.com.

The Simon & Schuster Speakers Bureau can bring authors to your live event.

For more information or to book an event contact the Simon & Schuster Speakers Bureau at 1-866-248-3049 or visit our website at www.simonspeakers.com.

Jacket designed by Heather Palisi

Interior designed by Mike Rosamilia

The text of this book was set in Adobe Caslon Pro.

Manufactured in the United States of America 0919 FFG

10 9 8 7 6 5 4 3 2 1

Library of Congress Cataloging-in-Publication Data

Names: Appleton, Victor, author.

Title: Restricted access / by Victor Appleton.

Description: First Aladdin hardcover/paperback edition. | New York : Aladdin, 2019. | Series: Tom Swift inventors' academy ; [3] | Summary: "Something seems amiss when an overnight lock-in at Swift Enterprises turns into a quarantine lockdown, and Tom and his friends must find the real reason behind it all"—Provided by publisher.

Identifiers: LCCN 2018053485 (print) | LCCN 2018057524 (eBook) |
ISBN 9781534436381 (eBook) | ISBN 9781534436367 (pbk) | ISBN 9781534436374 (hc)

Subjects: | CYAC: Inventors—Fiction. | Robbers and outlaws—Fiction. | Reporters and reporting—Fiction. | Friendship—Fiction. | Science fiction.

Classification: LCC PZ7.A652 (eBook) | LCC PZ7.A652 Rg 2019 (print) | DDC [Fic]—dc23

LC record available at https://lccn.loc.gov/2018053485

Contents

The Interrogation Frustration

I PADDED DOWN THE STAIRS AS QUIETLY AS possible. I slid one hand down the handrail with the other steadying the backpack slung over my shoulder. I tried to keep my school supplies from rattling, a sound that might give away my position. Luckily, school was already out for the day, and I didn't run into any other students along the way. I'm sure I looked as if I was up to something—which I was, of course.

When I reached the first floor, I peeked into the main hallway. Only a few students were in sight. A couple milled by lockers and one shuffled toward the front door. There was no sign of *him*, though.

I took a deep breath and stepped out. I kept a brisk but quiet pace as I made my way to the center of the building. Once at the main intersection, I could turn left toward the front entrance or I could turn right and head out through the back door. My plan, such as it was, was to take a right.

I mentally kicked myself for not coming up with a real plan. Instead of waiting behind in Engineering class, it would've been so much easier to leave after the final bell rang. Then I could simply blend in with the crowd of exiting students. Now I was out in the open, exposed.

As I neared the main junction, I could see into the hallway leading to the front entrance. I skidded to a stop.

There he was. Inside the school.

The tall man wore a dark blue blazer and jeans. His back was to me as he peered into the chess team's trophy case.

I exhaled and slowly began moving again. I shuffled down the corridor toward him. If I could just make it to the junction without being spotted, I could turn right and duck out through the back doors. Unfortunately, he must have spotted my reflection in the glass case. The man spun around as soon as I was near.

"Tom!" He held up a hand. His gray-speckled beard stretched across his face as he grinned.

I nodded and sighed. I hitched up my backpack, gave a weak smile, and walked over to him.

"Sorry." I jutted a thumb back down the hall. "I was just . . . uh . . ."

"It doesn't matter, you're here now," said Mr. Kavner. He ushered me toward the front door. "Let's sit on the front steps. Get some air."

Steven Kavner was a friend of my father's. Normally, not someone I'd want to avoid. But he was also a journalist who wanted to interview me for a story. *That* was something that I wished I could avoid.

Mr. Kavner and I sat on one of the long cement steps. "State your name, please," he said.

I cocked my head a little. "But . . . you already know my name."

Mr. Kavner grinned. He tapped the tiny body cam poking out of the front pocket on his blue blazer. "Yeah, but just for the record."

I sighed. "Tom Swift Junior."

"Great," said Mr. Kavner. "And where do you go to school?"

I glanced up at the school's name stretching across the building above us. He just pointed to the small camera again.

"The Swift Academy of Science and Technology," I replied.

Mr. Kavner nodded. "Tell me a little about your school."

I squirmed a bit and sighed again. "Well, it's a special school where we get to learn advanced subjects, create our own inventions, and go on cool field trips. Stuff like that."

I knew I was really underselling it. The academy was way more than that. Advanced subjects? How about aerodynamics and engineering to go along with algebra and history. Create our own inventions? It wouldn't be unusual to see robots or drones zipping through the halls. I would know; I piloted some of them. And as far as cool field trips were concerned, last year the eighth graders had a lock-in at the Wesley Observatory. Shandra Watts even discovered a comet.

Yeah, I knew my description didn't do the school justice, and Mr. Kavner knew it too. He rolled his eyes.

"Gee, Tom," he said with a wide grin. "I couldn't help but notice that you and your school share the same name."

I rubbed the back of my neck and shifted a bit on the hard step. "Yeah, my dad founded the school with the profits from his company, Swift Enterprises."

Of course, Mr. Kavner was well aware of this, too. After all, he and my father had gone to college together. They had even worked on some inventions together. But I guess somewhere along the way, Mr. Kavner's interests had changed. The only reason I had agreed to the interview was because he was a friend of my father's.

The thing is, I'm not too thrilled to share my name with the school. Don't get me wrong, I'm proud of my father and his accomplishments, especially the school. But all I've ever wanted was to be treated like any other student. And now I was the subject of a news story that would do the exact opposite. Needless to say, I really didn't want to be here.

"Can you tell me about your upcoming lock-in at Swift Enterprises?" Mr. Kavner asked.

I winced as a couple of fellow students exited the building. They gave us curious glances.

"Actually, can we finish this another time?" I said as I slowly stood. "My friends and I have to test something we're working on."

Mr. Kavner's eyes lit up. "A new invention?" He sprang to his feet. "Can I see?"

Oh boy. That was the wrong thing so say to a journalist.

I held out a hand. "Whoa, uh . . . it's not done yet. And it's not mine. I'm just helping. But when it's ready, sure."

His shoulders drooped. "Oh, okay." He reached up and pressed a button on the side of his body cam. "So, we'll pick it up tomorrow?"

I snatched up my backpack and bolted for the main door. "You bet!" I called back to him.

I felt a little bad brushing off Mr. Kavner like that. But I felt a lot worse being the focus of his article. You see, the worst thing about attending a school with your name on it was . . . well . . . attending a school with your name on it. Everyone automatically assumes you get special treatment. And I mean everyone: teachers, students, you name it. So when I first started here, I did everything I could to prove that I was just a regular student. I didn't expect special privileges or easy As. And I certainly didn't go crying to my father when something didn't go my way. And let me tell you, my father's default position would be to take a teacher's side anyway. So you can imagine my surprise when he asked me to talk to his reporter friend.

I made my way through the school and out the back door, and jogged down the sidewalk toward the track. The academy didn't have a track team or anything. We were more about our fencing team and killer chess team, but that didn't stop us from also having a state-of-the-art track. We mainly used it for running in gym class. Otherwise, the stadium only filled up when we had large outdoor assemblies where we watched fellow students launch model rockets, that sort of thing.

The track was mostly deserted. A couple of students sat in the bleachers and someone was actually speeding around the track. My three friends had started without me.

I set my pack down behind the two who were watching from the side. "What lap is this?" I asked.

"This is her second one," replied Noah Newton. My

best friend glanced down at his phone. His stopwatch app ticked away the seconds.

"She's not going as fast as she'd hoped," said Amy Hsu.

I dug through my pack and pulled out a small pair of binoculars. I uncapped the lenses and trained them on the girl zipping around the track. Samantha Watson came into focus. Her brown hair was pulled back in a ponytail, and she had traded out her glasses for her prescription sport goggles. The four of us made up the Formidable Foursome, as my dad liked to call us.

Sam sped around the track on what looked like a Segway on each foot. Each of her sneakers was strapped onto a platform with a large wheel on either side, and each skate had its own gyroscope that kept it level. But unlike the Segway, there was no handle and it wasn't self-propelled. Sam operated them like regular roller skates or Rollerblades. They were also connected wirelessly, so if they moved too far away from each other, they would subtly turn back. In theory, it would be difficult to wipe out while wearing them.

"Coming around the home stretch," Noah announced as Sam rounded the end of the track and headed toward us.

Sam wore kneepads, elbow pads, wrist guards, and a helmet, but none of the safety gear seemed to slow her down. She pumped her legs and swung her arms like a speed skater racing toward the finish line.

"Time!" Noah shouted as she zipped past us. He checked his phone. "One minute, point zero eight seconds."

Amy looked up and to the right. We all knew this expression well. When Amy looked up and to the right, she was accessing her mental calculator. And when she looked up and to the left, she was looking at her internal clock. It was spooky how accurate she was. "Average speed," Amy said, "thirty-five kilometers per hour."

"I know science is all about the metric system," said Noah. "But give me that in good old MPH, will ya?"

Only a brief glance up and to the right this time. "Almost twenty-two miles per hour," Amy replied.

"Wow," I said. "Impressive."

"Still . . . too . . . slow," Sam said between breaths as she rolled up to us. "It's . . . this track."

She had a point. I pressed a foot down and the track surface gave ever so slightly. See, this polyurethane track was made for running. It not only absorbed the impact of runners' steps, but the surface was also rough so runners could be safer in all kinds of weather. A smooth, firm track would be better for wheeled vehicles to get more traction. And more traction meant more speed. That's why race car tires have no tread at all—for more surface contact with the racetrack.

"I'll get more accurate results this weekend," Sam said with a grin. "I can't wait."

This Friday we were going to have our very first lock-in at my father's company next door, Swift Enterprises. One of the new employees came up with the idea and coordinated with our engineering instructor, Mr. Edge. The entire seventh grade would have access to the company's industrial equipment and testing areas. That included the company's indoor track. Which *was* designed for wheeled vehicles.

"You'll do great," I told Sam. "You look like you have the whole speed-skater form down."

Sam blotted her neck with a towel. "I think I could do better."

"You could ask Mrs. Scott for some advice," Amy suggested. "I think she used to be in a Roller Derby."

"News flash," said Noah. "I think she's *still* in a Roller Derby."

Amy covered her mouth. "No way."

Sam nodded. "I don't doubt it."

I clapped my hands together. "Okay, it's Sam's invention, so she got to go first. Who's next?"

"Sam *did* get the first turn," said Noah. "Then Amy and I got our turns. This was Sam's second run."

"What?" I asked. "Everyone's gone but me?"

"Hey, you had your big interview," Sam said. "We weren't going to wait forever."

"How did it go?" Amy asked.

Noah stepped between Amy and me. "No more questions for Mr. Swift, please." He placed a hand on my chest and jutted his other arm toward the girls. "And no autographs or selfies at this time."

Sam and Amy laughed while I just shook my head. My friends knew I didn't want to be a part of the news story. But if your friends can't give you grief about this stuff, who can?

I chuckled and pushed Noah's hand away. "It went . . . well . . . shorter than expected." I let out a breath. "We're not finished yet. I kind of just put it off."

"You might as well get it over with, Swift," Sam advised as she removed her safety gear. "Just rip that bandage right off." She handed me the wrist guards.

I strapped on the guards and put the interview out of my mind for now. I tried to replace the anxiety with excitement about trying the skates for the first time. Even though this was really Sam's invention, we each had a hand in it. I helped her design the suspension, Noah contributed big hunks of computer code for the wireless link, and Amy checked and double-checked Sam's calculations from possible speed to maximum body weight. Through all of the testing and retesting, I had yet to even try them on.

I pointed to the skates. "So how hard were they to control?"

"'Control' isn't really the right word," Sam replied. She removed the rest of her pads and helmet. "It's a little more intuitive than that."

"My mom tried to teach me ice skating when I was little," Amy said. "I was horrible at it."

"But she nailed these skates," said Noah. "You just have to go with the flow."

"'Going with the Flow' is my middle name," I said swimmingly. I finished putting on Sam's safety gear.

I was really good at that. Not strapping on safety

gear, but going with the flow. I often ran in with half a plan and figured out everything else on the fly. I was very meticulous when it came to science, but with most other things . . . yeah, I usually just winged it.

"Be careful with these," Sam said as she removed the skates from her shoes.

"I got this." I gave her a dismissive wave as I sat on the track. I quickly strapped the skates onto my shoes like I had done it a hundred times.

I'll admit I was cocky; I was a decent skater on my own set of Rollerblades. Heck, I hadn't even wiped out that time Noah and I used three fire extinguishers to propel us down the sidewalk.

I held my arms steady as I stood on the skates. My left foot was tipped down and my right was tipped up. I felt the gyroscopes push back as they leveled out both feet. Once I was stable, I leaned forward ever so slightly. I didn't fall over, but glided forward instead.

I grinned. "Cool!"

I tried to push off with my right foot, just as I would with regular skates. As I kicked out, I felt the wheels angle against my will, turning my right foot toward my left. The automatic movement surprised me and I pushed back instinctively. The skate didn't budge and I wobbled, my arms swinging wildly.

"You're fighting it, dude," Noah said.

"Just ease into it," Sam instructed.

I tried to push out again, this time not as far. Unfortunately, I leaned back too much and the skates began to roll backward.

"Does this thing come with training wheels?" Noah asked Sam.

I felt myself losing balance again and my arms waved some more. I knew the gyroscopes would keep me upright, but I couldn't convince my body of that. Then my right leg went out too far again and the wheels cut back automatically. I wobbled even more.

"You're trying too hard," said Amy.

She was right. I couldn't just go with it. I was trying too hard to control the situation and I was doing it very badly. So badly that my right foot cut in front of my left and my legs twisted together. I spun in a clumsy pirouette before slamming, butt-first, onto the track.

At that moment, I was glad the track had some give to it.

2

The Suppression Concession

AFTER NOAH'S MOTHER DROPPED ME OFF, I reheated some leftovers for dinner and went straight to my room. My dad wasn't home yet so I had the place to myself. After my mom died a few years ago, my dad had gone above and beyond trying to be two parents in one. He did his best to make sure we got to talk over dinner together. Of course, running a huge tech company didn't always allow for that, and he sometimes had to work late. And with the upcoming lock-in, I'm sure there was a mad push to complete some tasks before the facility was invaded by a bunch of twelve- and thirteen-year-olds.

That evening, my room was more of a mess than usual since I had several tools strewn about while working on my latest invention. My dad and I had come to an agreement a while back concerning the neatness of my room. As long as there were no dirty dishes and all my dirty laundry was in the hamper by the door, I could continue my very organized (but maybe chaotic-looking) *pile* system. But I couldn't stick with just a regular clothes hamper. Where's the fun in that? So I came up with my trebuchet.

A trebuchet is a fancy French word that means . . . a catapult that uses a counterweight to fling stuff a long distance. Okay, that's not really what it means. But that's *so* what it does! I had completed my homework and was putting the finishing touches on my laundry trebuchet.

It was mostly made of wood and stood about a meter tall in the back of my room. There was a large bucket attached at the end of its long arm to carry the payload (my laundry). I had also borrowed a few of my dad's free weights from his home gym to act as a counterweight. In theory, the trebuchet would fling my dirty clothes across the room to land in the hamper.

Now, I know that I didn't invent the trebuchet (I'm

sure that was some medieval French guy), but I did come up with a cool weight sensor. See, there's no point in just flinging every piece of dirty clothing one at a time. I added a sensor that would keep track of the amount of clothes in the bucket. Then, when it was full enough, it would trigger the mechanism and let fly!

I was in the middle of adding clothes to the bucket when I heard my dad enter the house.

"Tom, I'm home!" came his voice from downstairs.

I added a dirty T-shirt to the bucket. "Hey, Dad," I replied. A pair of jeans joined the shirt in the load.

I heard him coming up the stairs. Just in time to see my first test! My dad was very supportive of my inventions as long as they didn't interfere with my schoolwork. He did worry that I stretched myself too thin sometimes, but as long as I kept my grades up, he let me explore any and all interests that came my way.

"Check it out, Dad," I said as I added a pair of dirty socks. "You're just in time. . . ."

Click.

I miscalculated the weight and my trebuchet fired. The counterweights dropped and the bucket arm swung up.

"Aw, you missed it," I said.

My dad stepped into my bedroom doorway just as the entire load of dirty laundry flew across the room. I felt like I was watching it in slow motion, and as my clothes soared through the air, I realized two things. One: I didn't take into account the wind resistance and how it would separate the clothes in midair. They spread out like a stinky shotgun blast. And two: I miscalculated my aim. My laundry's flight path did not lead to the hamper beside the door. It led to the door itself.

My dad was pelted with dirty clothes. He held up his arms and tried to bat away an assault of dirty jeans and T-shirts. All in all, I think only one sock actually made it into the hamper. Its mate was draped across my father's face.

My father scowled and peeled it from his head.

"I'm sorry, Dad," I said, rushing forward. "My aim was way off. And my timing."

My father sighed. "I have five labs running a wide assortment of experiments," he replied. "And I have a few introverted employees less than thrilled with being inundated by a bunch of seventh graders. Right now, being contaminated with a teenager's dirty sock is the least of my worries." He dropped the sock into the nearby hamper. "That's not why I'm upset with you."

"What?" I asked. A knot grew in my stomach. He was really upset with me?

"Sit down, Tom," my father said. This was never good.

I plopped down on the bed while my father pulled over my desk chair. He sat down and looked me in the eye. "I spoke with Steve Kavner earlier today."

I glanced down and sighed. I should've seen this coming.

"Do you think the interview went well?" my dad asked.

"No," I admitted. "I . . . I kind of blew him off."

"Yeah, that's the impression he got too," my dad said. "Look, Tom, I thought we were going to make this work."

My father and I had already had this conversation when he first asked me to give the interview. He knew why I didn't want to do it and he made me do it anyway.

"*You* wanted to make this work," I said. "I didn't want to do it."

"But you said you would, so I expect you to honor your word," my dad replied.

"I answered some questions!" I said.

My dad raised an eyebrow. "You know what I mean."

I rubbed the back of my neck. "Yeah, but at school? With everyone there?"

"I know how you feel about being called out because you're my son," he said. "And I appreciate how you don't want any special treatment. I really do."

I wanted to tell my dad that *no*, he didn't know how it felt. His name was an asset. His name was part of the company's name. He was the boss. He was supposed to be special.

Of course, I didn't say any of that.

"This news article will be great publicity for the school," my dad continued. "We could get more funding, more students, maybe even expand."

"If it's about the school, why does it have to be me?" I asked.

My dad shrugged. "That's the angle Steve wanted to take. Besides, it's good to get out of your comfort zone sometimes, don't you think?"

I cocked my head at him. "Really?"

"Sure," he replied. "That's how we grow. Learn new things about ourselves."

That seemed like a weak argument, especially coming from my dad. "I guess," I said.

He put a hand on my shoulder. "Look, you do all kinds of things for your friends, right?"

"Sure," I said.

"Well, Steve's my friend." His face softened. "And just between you and me, I get the feeling that he really needs this story."

"He needs it?" I asked. I didn't know what that meant. I *needed* to be left out of the article.

"I think so," my dad said. "It's hard being a freelancer, especially when supporting a family. I even offered him a job at Swift Enterprises. He was a brilliant researcher when we were in college." My father leaned back in the chair. "He turned me down. But he did ask for press access to the academy."

"Yeah, but why does he need me?" I asked.

"He said he wants a subject to follow," my dad replied. "To see the school through someone's eyes."

I still didn't like it, but I could see my dad's point. He was just trying to help out a friend. I would certainly do the same for any of my friends.

"Come on, Tom," my dad said. "It won't take that

long. Then your time in the spotlight will be over, and you can go back to being a regular student."

I sighed. "All right."

My dad stood and patted my shoulder. "Thanks. And remember, stepping out of your comfort zone is good once in a while."

"I guess so," I murmured.

I could think of better ways to step out of my comfort zone. Testing new inventions, not knowing if they would work or not. Except, I did that kind of stuff all the time anyway. I guess that *was* my comfort zone.

"I knew I could count on you," my dad said as he walked toward the door. "Just answer his questions honestly and let him follow you around for a couple of days."

I glanced up. "A couple of *days*?"

My dad stepped through the doorway. "He's going to the lock-in tomorrow night too."

I shook my head. Great. Not only would I have to deal with a reporter shadowing me at school, he'd also be looking over my shoulder during the lock-in. All . . . night . . . long?

I sat upright. "Wait, what?"

The Intrusion Collusion

WHEN I ARRIVED AT SCHOOL THE NEXT DAY, THE
front hallway looked like a collection site for a clothing drive, or the staging area for a hurricane evacuation.
Gym bags, sleeping bags, and big plastic bins lined both
sides of the hall. Most of the academy students were
attending the lock-in that night and were dropping
their stuff off in the front hall. As more students arrived,
they excitedly added their gear to the piles.

I remember when I had been excited about the
lock-in. I mean, who wouldn't be? Get out of school early
on Friday and then spend the night in a cutting-edge

facility, with access to most of their high-tech equipment. Need an electron microscope to test a hypothesis or two? Swift Enterprises has you covered. Need to test a prototype's aerodynamics in an actual wind tunnel? No problem there. Personally, I was going to use the company's circuit printer to make a bunch of different circuit boards for my projects. Except now I'd have to do it with a reporter in tow.

I spotted a large bin with S. WATSON printed on the top. I assumed it was full of Sam's prototype skates as well as spare parts and previous versions of her invention. I sighed, plopped my own gym bag next to her bin, and trudged to class. The thought of having a reporter looking over my shoulder all night had deflated my excitement.

My algebra classroom was half full by the time I arrived, and Amy and Sam were already in their seats. Sam leaned over and was pointing to something on Amy's bulky sweater. Sam whipped her hand back when she noticed me, and Amy sat up straight. I raised my eyebrows questioningly at them.

"Uh, hey," I said as I took my seat in front of Sam.

"Hi, Tom," Amy greeted.

"Are you sore from yesterday?" asked Sam. A sly smile stretched across her face. They were never going to let me forget about my unfortunate landing on the track.

"Ha ha, I'm just fine," I replied, though I did feel a dull twinge when I sat on the desk. I wasn't about to tell them that.

"Well, if you want to redeem yourself, I want to try them out again in the gym during lunch," Sam said. "I'd like to get the feel of a hard surface before running the Swift Enterprises track."

"I'll just watch," I said observantly. No sense in falling down on a harder surface *and* have it happen in front of a news reporter.

"I'll try again," Noah said as he slid into his desk in front of Amy.

Amy glanced down at her sweater. "Not today, thank you," she told Sam. Then the two girls exchanged a knowing smile. My brow furrowed as I glanced from Sam to Amy. There was some kind of inside joke there.

I was about to ask what was going on when Amy sat up in her seat and looked straight ahead. The three of us followed suit. We knew Amy well enough to read her body language by now. Her internal clock told her it was almost time for first period to begin. The bell rang, proving her accuracy once more.

I glanced around the classroom. There was no sign of Mr. Kavner. I didn't dare hope that he had changed his mind. But I couldn't help myself.

Our algebra teacher, Mr. Jenkins, rose from his desk, his long gray ponytail swishing behind him. "Because of tonight's lock-in, I'm not assigning homework."

A wave of approval rippled through the class. Evan Wittman even clapped.

Mr. Jenkins raised a finger, silencing everyone. "But . . . that just means we have more ground to cover today."

Then moans washed through.

"Turn to page eighty-four of your text," Mr. Jenkins continued, "and we'll begin with . . ."

A loud tone sounded from the PA system. "Mr. Jenkins?" asked Ms. Lane from the front office.

One of the perks of the academy was all the upgraded tech that came built into the classrooms. This, of course, extended to our two-way PA system. "Yes?" Mr. Jenkins replied.

"Please send Tom Swift to the office," she said.

The students gave a collective "oooooh" as Mr. Jenkins nodded in my direction.

As I got up from my desk, Amy's stomach gave a loud growl. I mean loud enough to hear over the oohing students. Sam and Amy giggled at the sound.

That was weird. Amy was one of the shyest people I knew. Her face usually turned bright red with embarrassment when the tiniest of snorts escaped while laughing. I would've thought that if her stomach growled that loudly, her entire head would explode. Instead, she just laughed it off.

Maybe finally making the fencing team had given her some confidence after all. Or . . . there was something my friends weren't telling me.

I caught Noah's eye to see if he knew the inside joke. He merely shrugged.

As I made my way to the front office, I knew Mr. Kavner's absence was too good to be true. That had to be why I was being called. Meeting him after school was one thing, but having a reporter follow me around school had to be by special permission. It was hard to believe our principal, Mr. Davenport, would like the idea.

A smile pulled at my lips. Maybe Mr. Davenport had vetoed the idea of having some strange man tail me all day. The disruption alone would be enough to turn him off the idea. My father may have set up the academy, but he never interfered with its curriculum or day-to-day operation. In the end, Mr. Davenport always had the final say. It felt as if a weight had been pulled off my chest. I would get out of the news story without being at fault.

I entered the front office and approached the reception desk. Ms. Lane didn't look up from her computer screen. "Mr. Davenport's office," she said, jutting a thumb over her shoulder.

"Yes, ma'am," I said, maybe a little too cheerfully.

I walked past her desk and turned into the principal's office. Mr. Davenport and Mr. Kavner stood behind the big oak desk, their backs to me. Mr. Davenport was pointing to a plaque on the wall. "This was my commendation from the school board."

I knocked on the open door. "Mr. Davenport?"

Both men turned and grinned. "Tom! Come in, come in," said the principal.

I felt the weight begin to press on my chest again.

Mr. Davenport was in way too good of a mood. He usually called me Mr. Swift. He hardly ever called any student by his or her first name.

"You wanted to see me, sir?" I asked.

"This is exciting news!" The principal beamed. "This article is going to be great for the school."

There it was. The weight was all the way back now.

"Uh, yeah," I said. I tried sounding enthusiastic, but my heart was plummeting to my feet.

Mr. Kavner held out both hands. "Now, I know you're not exactly thrilled being the focus of this story."

Mr. Davenport cocked his head. "Really? Don't you want to be famous? You share a name with the school. Who better to represent it?"

I shrugged. "I guess so."

"Look," said Mr. Kavner. "I spoke with your dad last night and Mr. Davenport today, and I think we've come up with a pretty good compromise."

"Really?" I asked. "What's that?"

Mr. Kavner held up a finger and then motioned toward the corner of the office. "Ro? Come here, buddy."

I hadn't seen the younger boy standing in the corner of the office examining Mr. Davenport's model of the

Mercury rocket. He wore a black T-shirt, had scruffy blond hair, and looked to be about ten years old. He left the display case and joined his father.

"This is my son, Rowan," said Mr. Kavner. He ruffled his son's hair. "Rowan, this is the guy I told you about. Tom."

Rowan gave a quick wave.

"Uh . . . hi," I said, waving back.

"Instead of me following you around all day"— he glanced at Mr. Davenport—"we thought Rowan might be a little less distracting. Then he could report back to me."

I wasn't going to be followed around by a strange man anymore. I was going to be a babysitter instead. I forced a smile. "Great."

This day was getting better and better.

4

The Adolescent Incident

"WAS THAT A REAL ROCKET?" ROWAN ASKED AS we walked back to my algebra class.

"What?" I asked.

"I mean, I know it wasn't a real rocket," said Rowan. "But was it the kind that can fly? Like a model rocket?"

"No, I think it was just a model-that-you-look-at rocket," I said.

"My dad and I made a model Mercury rocket too," he explained. "But it was the kind that could fly. It was a Mercury-Redstone."

I was impressed. The kid already knew about the

Mercury rockets, from NASA's first manned mission to space.

"We get to launch model rockets here sometimes," I told him.

"I thought so," he said. "You can't be a science school without model rockets."

He continued chattering as we walked to Mr. Jenkins's class.

"I got to see a real Mercury rocket one time," Rowan said as we reached the door. "My dad had a meeting at NASA in Houston and we got to . . ."

"Uh, hey," I interrupted, putting my hand on the classroom door. "We have to be quiet now. Class has already started."

"Oh, okay," Rowan whispered.

I opened the door slowly, hoping not to disturb Mr. Jenkins's lecture. However, a low murmur flowed through the open doorway. We peeked inside to see the entire class crowded around Amy. Even Mr. Jenkins peered over the top of everyone's heads.

I moved into the crowd to see what was wrong. Amy didn't enjoy being the center of attention. Was she ill? Or hurt?

As I neared her, I saw that the attention wasn't on Amy after all, but on a tiny gray Chihuahua. Its head poked out of her unzipped sweater as several students reached in to gently pet it.

Amy noticed my look of surprise. "His name is Otis," she said. "I'm bringing him tonight for a custom fitting."

Amy's plan was to use the Swift industrial 3-D printers at the lock-in. She had spent the past couple of weeks visiting animal shelters around town. Her aim was to make prosthetic limbs and carts for dogs and cats that needed them, to help them get adopted.

Sure, we had a 3-D printer at school, but the Swift Enterprises printers could create objects in finer detail. They could also print things using materials other than plastic.

Sam gave the tiny dog a scratch behind the ears. "Otis can't use his back legs," she explained. "Amy's going to make a little cart for him."

I glanced at Noah. "Did you know about this?" I asked.

Noah shook his head. He could barely move with all the students pushed in around him. "No one did," he replied. "Little guy started barking right after you left."

Amy gave a nervous smile. "I thought he'd stay quiet in my sweater and not be disruptive."

That explained Amy's growling "stomach" from before.

Noah glanced up at the crowd of people and grinned. "How's that working out for you?"

"Okay, people," Mr. Jenkins said. "Now that you've gotten that out of your systems, return to your desks, please."

I slid into my desk as everyone went back to theirs.

"And it looks as if Miss Hsu isn't the only one who brought a guest today," Mr. Jenkins continued.

I glanced around the room and realized everyone was looking at me. I totally forgot about the kid.

I got to my feet. "Uh, this is Rowan." I turned and gestured to the ten-year-old hovering by the classroom door. "He's going to hang out with me today to ... uh ... learn about the school."

Rowan looked up from his feet long enough to give a nervous wave. I knew how he felt.

"Welcome, Rowan," said Mr. Jenkins. "You can have a seat in one of the chairs in the back." Our teacher returned to the math problem projected onto the electronic board. "As you can see ..."

SKREEEAAAAAAAPE!

A loud scraping sound came from the back of the classroom. Everyone turned to see Rowan pushing one of the chairs forward. He slowly pushed it down the aisle with a couple of the students having to scoot their desks to either side to make room.

SKREEEAAAAAAAPE!

Rowan finally got the chair next to mine. He side-stepped between it and Noah's desk before plopping down. Mr. Jenkins and the rest of us continued to stare.

Rowan jutted a thumb at me. "I'm supposed to stay with Tom all day."

Mr. Jenkins raised an eyebrow. "Okay . . . as I was saying . . ."

I didn't hear the rest of the sentence as I sighed and rubbed my forehead. This was going to be a long half-day.

Rowan did surprisingly well sitting through algebra, for a ten-year-old. He didn't fidget or fall asleep or anything. I can't say that I would've been as good at that age. At least my next class, history, was more interesting for him. We happened to be covering the space race, and we were just getting into the Russian cosmonauts and American astronauts. I knew he was interested in that subject. And to top it all off, I had robotics class right after. What ten-year-old doesn't like robots? I was hoping Rowan would be so excited about his time at the academy that his father would want to change the angle of the story, maybe write from his son's point of view instead.

I was feeling much better about everything when Rowan and I met up with Sam, Amy, and Noah at lunch.

Amy still had Otis with her. But since the cat was out of the bag, so to speak (or the dog out of the sweater), she didn't try to hide him anymore. It turned out that Otis was sitting in a small pack against Amy's chest. It was strapped over her shoulders like a little backpack, but in reverse.

"What do you think of our school?" Sam asked Rowan.

His face lit up. "It's really cool. I hope I get to come here someday. Do you really get to invent stuff?"

"All the time," said Noah. "That's what tonight's lock-in is all about."

"What's your invention?" Rowan asked.

Noah pulled his phone from his pocket. "I came up with this app that maps the inside of buildings in real time." He turned on his phone and pulled up the app. "It uses the camera to photograph the hallways, stairs, and even names on doors."

"What for?" asked Rowan.

"Well, if you do get to come to the academy, you can use my app to find your way around," he explained. "All you have to do is walk the entire building, taking pics of everything. Then, later on, you can tell it you want to go to . . . say, physics class. Then the app will tell you the easiest way to get there."

"He's already mapped the entire school," Amy added.

"Several times over," said Noah. "But I want to map the hallways of Swift Enterprises. I don't know that building as well, so it should be a good scientific test."

"But I thought there was top secret stuff in there," said Rowan.

"My dad had everyone lock away any 'proprietary developments,' as he calls them," I explained. "That way, all the kids can have access to the equipment without stumbling across secret stuff."

"What's your invention?" Rowan asked Amy.

She told him about her plans to use the Swift Enterprises 3-D printer to help some of the shelter animals.

Rowan reached over to pet Otis. "I bet he's going to love that."

"I hope so," said Amy.

"What about you, Tom?" asked Rowan.

Noah made snoring noises. "Snoozefest!"

"Hey," I said. "It's an important part of the process." I went on to explain how I would spend my time printing circuit boards for various inventions I had going.

"What kind of inventions?" asked Rowan.

"Well . . ." I thought for a moment. "Here's one. But you can't tell your dad. I don't want the whole world to know about it yet."

"Okay," said Rowan. He reached to his chest and pressed a small device poking out of his shirt pocket. Since both the device and his T-shirt were black, I hadn't noticed it until now.

"Dude, what is that?" Noah asked, pointing at Rowan's chest.

I shook my head. I knew exactly what it was. "It's his dad's body cam," I replied.

Sam straightened up, her eyes narrowing. "You've been recording us this whole time?"

Amy immediately looked to her lap.

"It's for my dad's story," Rowan replied.

Noah grinned and patted down his hair. "So we'll get to be in the story too? Cool!"

Rowan shrugged. "I don't know. Maybe."

So much for Rowan being the focus of the story. Mr. Kavner wasn't going to tell it from his son's point of view. Instead, he just sent along a little cameraman to record my every move.

"So, what's the invention?" asked Rowan.

"It's . . . uh . . ." I'd lost all enthusiasm. "Well, one of them is an alarm clock where you have to solve mathematical equations to shut it off."

"I told him I could help him make an app for his phone that would do the same thing," said Noah.

"Yeah, but I don't get to burn my own circuit boards for an app," I replied.

"It sounds hard," Rowan said.

"You get multiple-choice answers," I explained. "But

you have to solve three equations in all, and they get harder as you go. Makes sure you're wide-awake by the time you're done."

Amy grinned. "I'd buy that."

Noah shook his head. "You better build in shock-proof housing, because I would *so* fling that thing across the room."

Rowan turned to Sam. "What about your invention?"

"So I built . . ." Sam began. She paused as Rowan pressed the switch on the body cam. "You're just going to turn that thing back on like it's no big deal, huh," she murmured.

"Oh." Rowan glanced around. "Is yours top secret too?"

"No, I mean—I don't know," Sam stammered. "I'm just not comfortable being recorded all the time."

Amy nodded in agreement.

Noah leaned closer to Sam and flashed the camera a peace sign. "Come on, Sam. You're no stranger to fame."

Sam had her own brush with fame when she invented a new water-sourcing method for drought-ridden areas. She had been interviewed multiple times and even got a scholarship to the academy because of it.

"Yeah," I agreed with Noah. "It's no big deal, right? Just rip that bandage right off."

Sam shot me a look before taking a deep breath. Then she told Rowan about her new skates and how she planned to test them on the company's indoor track.

"Cool!" said Rowan. "Can I try them?"

Sam shrugged. "Okay. I was going to try them out in the gym before the lock-in."

We dumped our trays and headed down to the gym. Sam detoured to the front hallway to grab her rolling plastic tote containing her skates and equipment. Once she was back, she handed out the safety gear to Rowan.

"Have you been on roller skates before?" asked Sam.

Rowan nodded his head vigorously. "And Roller-blades, and ice skates!" He began strapping on the pads.

"Better be careful," Noah warned. He clapped a hand on my shoulder. "Tom found out the hard way that we don't have safety gear for everything."

Rowan sat on the gym floor while Sam knelt and strapped the skates to the bottom of his feet.

Amy glanced at me nervously. "Will you get in trouble if you break him?" And I swear, Otis gave the slightest of whines.

Noah and Sam each took one of Rowan's hands and helped him up. "Be careful," Sam warned. "Just start off slow."

"And remember, when you feel the skates self-correcting, don't fight it," Noah added. "Isn't that right, Tom?"

I shook my head. "I don't want to hear it, Noah."

Noah and Sam let go of Rowan. He wobbled a bit but smiled anyway. Then he began moving forward. Slowly at first, he kicked one foot out and then another. The wobbling stopped and he glided smoothly across the gym floor.

"Great job," said Sam.

Amy let out a sigh of relief.

"This is so cool!" Rowan shouted.

Noah walked back over to me and grinned. "You really don't like this kid, do you?"

"I really don't like this kid," I replied.

5

The Conduction Introduction

OKAY, THAT WASN'T TRUE. I LIKED ROWAN JUST fine. He seemed like a great kid, and we even shared many of the same interests. I just didn't like the idea of him being around recording my every move. And him being better than me with Sam's skates was just the cherry on top of a melted ice cream sundae.

"He's even better than I was on my first try," said Sam.

I smirked. "Yeah, that's great."

A long tone blasted from the school's intercom.

"Attention, Swift Academy seventh graders," Mr.

Davenport's voice echoed out of the gym speakers. "Those going on the field trip, please make your way to the front of the school."

Rowan stripped off his skates and gear and we helped Sam pack everything into her tote. We left the gym and joined the steady stream of students flowing toward the front of the building. Everyone picked up their bags, backpacks, and supplies from the main hallway and poured out into the front parking lot.

The teachers who were chaperoning the lock-in did their best to keep everyone gathered together. Mr. Edge from engineering and Mrs. Scott from robotics seemed to take the lead. I also spotted Mr. Kavner standing with the rest of the teachers as my dad predicted. It wasn't long before the organized chaos shepherding that many students was a bit more organized and less chaotic.

"All right, everyone," said Mr. Edge. "Let's move out!"

The group funneled into a wide line and crossed the street. Since it was a private road shared by the academy and Swift Enterprises, there was no traffic to worry about. And since the offices were so close, there was no need for a cramped bus ride for this field trip. We marched toward the looming office building like an army preparing to storm a castle.

Everyone entered through the many glass doors and filed into the huge reception lobby. Luckily it was big enough to hold everyone, but just barely. The students crowded in among gleaming marble columns and walls.

Just under the high ceiling, the Swift Enterprises logo hung above everyone's heads. My mom had helped design that logo. It was a giant *SE*, but the *E* was shaped like a wing, giving the logo a sense of motion.

Several company employees were scattered about, awaiting our arrival. Each of them held up a sign labeling their department.

"Okay, peeps," said Mrs. Scott. "You know the drill. Find your division and get in line."

"Whoa," Rowan said, glancing at all the signs. "There's a wind tunnel here? And a robotics lab?"

"Pretty sweet, huh?" said Noah. He held up his phone and made a wide, sweeping motion. "And with my new app, you'll soon be able find your way around this vast scientific citadel."

I gave him a look. "Since when do you use the word '*citadel*'?"

Noah shrugged. "What? All the time." He glanced at Rowan and I understood then—he was playing it up for the body cam.

I shook my head and pointed to a woman holding a circuit-printing sign. "There's ours," I told Rowan. I turned to my friends. "I'll swing by and check on you later."

"Okay, good luck," said Amy. She snaked her way toward a man holding a 3-D printing sign.

Sam started heading to a woman holding a test track sign.

"I'll hang with you guys until it clears out," said Noah. He tapped the screen on his phone, bringing up his app. "I'm going to start in the lobby anyway."

"Is there a bathroom here?" Rowan asked.

I pointed to the opposite end of the lobby. "It's over there. Don't forget what line we're in."

After Rowan had disappeared into the crowd, Noah nudged me. "Are you trying to get him lost?"

"He'll be fine," I said.

At least, I hoped he wouldn't get lost. Even though I wasn't thrilled about him tagging along all night, I wouldn't want to lose him in the huge facility. I don't think my dad would be happy about that.

Once most everyone had been divided into groups, a thin young man wearing a shiny blue suit and red tie appeared and slid a chair toward the large reception desk. He hopped onto the chair and then stepped onto the desk.

"Hello, everyone, and welcome to Swift Enterprises!" the man shouted.

There was a smattering of applause.

"I'm James Brodigan from the public relations department." He scanned the crowd. "Now, when I suggested this lock-in to Mr. Swift, I wanted him to be the one welcoming you today. Unfortunately, he was called away to a special meeting and will be back later. What kind of meeting, you ask? Well, I could tell you . . ." He glanced around suspiciously. "But I'd have to kill you."

A few chuckles escaped the crowd. Mr. Brodigan glanced around expectantly.

"Just kidding." He gave a dismissive wave. "No, he delegated this auspicious task to me. Even though I've only been with the company for two weeks and I can't stand children."

Everyone glanced at each other, confused.

"Kidding! I'm kidding. Another joke," the man said. "I've actually been here *three* weeks."

This time everyone laughed.

"Now, a couple of things before you're off on your adventure. Even though this is a highly secure area, you may have noticed that you weren't made to give up your phones."

He was right. Usually visitors had to leave their phones at the front desk to keep someone from photographing top secret projects. I had personal experience when it came to this. Even the boss's son didn't get excluded from that rule.

"I know how much you kids can't live without your phones. So, the good news is we've locked away all sensitive material. Feel free to take as many selfies as you like." He held up a finger. "But the bad news is . . . you'll have to wait until you leave before posting them or sending them to friends. The entire building is shielded so no signals get in or out."

That meant no texts or calls. There was some rumbling in the crowd at that.

"And the last thing . . ." Mr. Brodigan waved his hands with a flourish. "I got my hands on the boss's corporate credit card, which means . . . all-you-can-eat pizza for dinner!"

Everyone applauded. Noah jammed his fingers in the corners of his mouth and gave a loud whistle.

"Now go have fun!" Mr. Brodigan finished. He climbed off the desk as the students began to file out of the lobby.

The groups who had business on the second or third floor took the stairs. Some of the larger groups headed toward the service elevator in the back. The rest of us who would work on the fourth or fifth floor waited in line for the regular elevator.

I noticed Mr. Kavner looking my way, but he kept his word and didn't hover over my shoulder. He ended up filing out with one of the other groups. Of course, there was no need to hover; he had Rowan to keep an eye on me.

Speaking of . . . I craned my neck to look past the remaining students. I couldn't see him anywhere.

"Okay, I'll see you later," Noah said as he raised his phone. The crowd had thinned enough for him to begin photographing the lobby.

"Ooh, our first spy!" Mr. Brodigan said as he drifted over. "What's your name?" He glanced at me, winked, and then pretended to block his mouth so Noah couldn't hear. "So I'll know what to tell the FBI."

"I'm Noah," said my friend. "And I'm working on a mapping app." He explained how his new invention would map the Swift Enterprises facility.

"Well if you need a beta tester, call me," said Brodigan. "I could use something like that." He shook his head. "I'm still getting lost in this place."

Noah chuckled. "You got it."

Mr. Brodigan turned to me, eyebrows raised. "And you are?"

Wait a minute . . . he didn't know who I was. Everyone at the academy and most of the company employees knew my name. It felt weird being anonymous for a change, but definitely not in a bad way.

"Uh . . ." I extended a hand. "My friends call me T."

Noah gave me a weird look but didn't blow my cover.

Mr. Brodigan shook my hand. "Well, T, glad you could make it." He turned to leave. "You kids try not to blow up the facility. I hear it's quite expensive."

After the man was out of earshot, Noah leaned forward. "What was that all about?"

I replied, "He doesn't know who I am."

"Who doesn't know who you are?" asked Rowan. I almost jumped. The kid had snuck up on me.

"One of the new employees," I replied.

"Why does that matter?" asked Rowan.

I tried to explain to Rowan how I didn't like special treatment at the school or from my father's employees. Actually, most of the employees treated me just fine. But there were a couple who fawned over me because I was the boss's kid. It was sickening, really. It was as if they could earn points with my dad by making me like them. I know I had just met the man, but Mr. Brodigan definitely seemed like fawner material.

"Why wouldn't you want special treatment?" asked Rowan.

"Forget it, man," Noah said, shaking his head. "I ask him that all the time."

The elevator dinged and opened ahead of us. "Our turn," said Mr. Smith, our group's leader. McKee Smith was a stout older man with a bushy gray mustache and had been with my dad's company since the beginning. I liked Mr. Smith. He definitely wasn't one of the fawners.

"See you later," I told Noah as we boarded the elevator with the rest of our group.

Noah gave a wave over his shoulder as he continued to photograph the lobby.

There were only six of us in our group, so the elevator ride wasn't crowded at all. When the doors opened on the fifth floor, we followed Mr. Smith down a long corridor.

We turned a corner and Rowan nearly tripped over one of the company's bright yellow robots.

"Whoa," he said, coming to a stumbling stop.

"Oh man, I should've warned you about those," I said.

The robot was the size of a small backpack, and slowly backed away from Rowan's feet. It was also *shaped* like a backpack, with a sloped, rounded front, square back end, and a black stripe crossing its center.

"What is that?" asked Rowan.

"That's one of my dad's B-bots," I replied. "They constantly vacuum the floors. And late at night, they wash and buff them too." I motioned for Rowan to step away. "Watch this."

Once we had moved away from the robot and its path was clear, it rolled forward. It turned the corner and continued its cleaning pattern down the hallway.

"Cool," said Rowan.

"They can sense when their path is blocked and stop." I pointed to a nearby opening in the wall. It was shaped like a half circle and looked like an oversize cartoon mouse hole. "They go in there to recharge and dump their dustbins."

"He invented those?" asked Rowan.

"Well, he's not the first to invent automatic vacuum cleaners," I admitted. "But he's the first to design a system that manages a whole office building."

We caught up with the rest of the group as they reached a set of glass security doors. A guard I didn't recognize sat at a desk on the other side. He reached under his desk and buzzed us in.

BUZZZZ-KLAK!

Once we were through the doors, we crossed the small entryway toward another closed door. Mr. Smith used a key card to open it and stepped to the side as we filed through.

We entered a dimly lit room with five computer consoles lined up against a large glass window. Through the window was a larger, brightly lit room full of huge printers, etchers, and drillers. Long conveyor belts connected the machines to each other. A steady hum emanated from the huge, boxlike equipment.

"All right, gang," said Mr. Smith. "As many of you

may know, you give me your board designs, I plug them into the computer, and then the machines over there spit them out. And be advised that I'm well aware that that is an oversimplified description of the process."

The group laughed.

"Now, is this anyone's first time?"

The group glanced around and Rowan tentatively raised his hand. Mr. Smith waved him over to the window and pointed out each piece of equipment. He showed him the huge screen printers that printed out the designs, the etchers that etched the circuit onto the board, and the driller that made precision holes into each board where needed.

"All right," said Mr. Smith. "Who's first?"

Jacob Mahaley stepped forward and held out a thumb drive.

"Good to see you again, Jake," said Mr. Smith. "If you like, I can double-check your circuit designs to see you don't have any shorts or broken connections."

"Yes, please," Jacob replied.

I'm sure not all of the company employees enjoyed working with kids, but Mr. Smith seemed to. Not only did he come to our school to give talks on circuitry, but he had also printed circuit boards for many of the students in the past.

While Jacob's circuit appeared on the computer screen, Rowan let out a long breath.

"I know this isn't the most exciting part of the company," I said. "But it's very helpful."

"What do you mean?" asked Rowan.

"Let me show you," I said revealingly, sliding off my backpack.

I unzipped my pack and removed one of the plastic, static-free envelopes. I opened it and slid out my alarm clock circuit board. It was fifteen by thirty centimeters, about the size of a clipboard.

"This is the circuit board for my alarm clock," I explained. "I made it at home."

"You made this yourself?" asked Rowan.

"With my dad, yeah," I replied. "It's not that hard."

I plugged in a battery and hit the power switch. A small LCD screen came to life.

"That's so cool that you made this," said Rowan.

"Thanks," I replied. "Now here's what happens when the alarm goes off."

I pressed the button that simulated the alarm, and a

mathematical equation appeared on the left side of the screen. Three answers appeared on the right. There was a button on the circuit board beside each answer.

"'What's twelve times four?'" Rowan read. "That's not so hard."

"Right," I said, pressing the button next to the answer: forty-eight. "But the next two equations get harder, to make sure you're awake."

The next equation appeared. It asked for the square root of 1,764.

"Wow," said Rowan. "What happens when you get a wrong answer?"

I shrugged. "You have to start all over again."

"I bet you're awake by then," said Rowan.

I held up the board. "The point is, picture this circuit board in an alarm clock."

"That's a big clock," said Rowan.

"Right," I replied. "Well, with the machines here, I can create one that's only about five by fifteen centimeters."

Rowan wrinkled his brow. "How big is that?"

I laughed. "About two by six inches."

Understanding crossed Rowan's face. "Oh. Cool!"

We waited in line while the rest of the group printed their boards. When it was my turn, I dug out my own thumb drive and handed it to Mr. Smith.

"How many today, Tom?" he asked with a grin.

I smiled. "Only four this time," I replied. "I was just showing Rowan a prototype I made at home." I turned around and Rowan was no longer standing behind me. "Rowan?" I scanned the room.

He was gone.

6

The Isolation Activation

I STEPPED OUT OF THE LAB AND SCANNED THE
entryway. Rowan wasn't in sight. Neither was the security guard. My stomach tightened. Maybe he got in trouble somehow and was snatched up by the guard. I knew that Rowan was supposed to be watching me, but being older, I felt responsible for him.

I pushed through the glass doors. Luckily, they weren't locked if anyone needed to get out.

"Rowan?" I shouted as I jogged down the empty hallway. With most of the staff either gone for the day or helping the students, I didn't have to worry about disturbing anyone's work. "Rowan?"

Another B-bot exited the wall and quietly rolled past me. Since I hadn't blocked its path, it ignored me as it worked.

I retraced our steps, heading for the elevator. Maybe Rowan tried to find something more exciting than printing circuit boards. I slowed, opening a few doors along the way. Empty offices and cubicle bays stared back at me. Rowan was nowhere in sight.

I tried a few more before turning a corner. Then several feet down the corridor, I spotted a door ajar.

"Rowan?" I called out.

I thought I heard an answer but it seemed faint and distant. As I moved closer and peeked through the open door, I realized why.

I pulled open the door to one of the anechoic chambers. The room had spherical walls so it was like standing in a large ball. It also had long foam pyramids covering the walls, ceiling, and most of the floor. The soft black spikes made it feel as if you were standing inside a giant cactus turned inside out. Rowan stood in the center of the room.

"Is this cool, or what?" he asked. Although there was excitement in his voice, the tone sounded muted. "What is this place?"

"It's called an anechoic chamber. My father helped design it. It's made to deaden sound," I replied, my voice coming out dull and muffled. I pointed to the ceiling. "The foam spikes absorb noise so none of it bounces off the walls or ceiling. There's no echo at all. They use it to test microphones, speakers, stuff like that."

"That's why my voice sounds so weird," he said as he gazed above. Then he gave a loud "Whoooop!" Although his volume was louder, his voice was a little flat. He giggled.

I felt a pang of guilt. It wasn't Rowan's fault that his father had made him tag along with me today. And it certainly wasn't his fault that I had chosen a boring project for the lock-in. Well, boring to most people, anyway. My dad's company was way more exciting than what I'd shown him so far. If a simple sound lab impressed him, he would love some of the other things going on around here.

"Come on," I said. "It's time I gave you a tour of Swift Enterprises."

I knew just the place to start. We hit the elevator and went down a couple of floors. When we got out, I led the way down the long corridor. Rowan was fascinated by another B-bot going about its duties.

We turned a corner and entered the suite housing Swift Enterprises' two electron microscopes. A group of students gathered around Dr. Reynolds. The woman wore a white lab coat and sat in front of a large video monitor. The image on the screen made it look as if the students were watching a science fiction movie. There was a ghastly alien creature that looked like a giant worm, with eight stubby legs near the front of its body. It had no eyes and a clawlike mouth.

"What is that?" Rowan asked as we joined the other students.

Dr. Reynolds pointed at the monitor. "This handsome fella is a microscopic Demodex mite." She nodded at Alicia Wilkes, who was standing in the center of the group. "It's from one of Alicia's skin scrapings."

Rowan's eyes widened and he took a step back as if she were contagious. The other students laughed.

Dr. Reynolds smiled. "Don't worry. You have them too," she said, pointing to Rowan. "We all do. They live on our faces." She blew a loose strand of dark hair from her face. "I didn't really have time for my research *and* to prepare something for this lock-in, so . . . I thought I'd let you bring the specimens to me."

Dr. Reynolds went on to explain how these mites don't actually poop, but save it all up until they die. Pretty gross, but Rowan was enthralled.

We left the group to continue their weird microscopic journey and headed down to one of the company's fabrication shops. The huge room was filled with every kind of industrial machine that chopped, welded, grinded, cut, and fused. The air was warm and thick with metallic odors.

We joined a group of students in one of the observation bays. They stood behind specially shielded glass as automated welders assembled various angled aluminum pipes.

"What's that?" asked Rowan.

One of the older students, Jim Mills, turned around and grinned. "It's going to be a roll cage."

Roll cages were the protective cages used on race cars and dune buggies. They protected the driver in case the vehicle were to roll over—hence the name.

Curiosity got the better of me. "What for?" I asked him.

Jim shook his head. "You'll find out at the next invention convention," he replied. Then he thought for a moment. "Or . . . maybe the one after that."

Mr. Edge hosted a showcase every month where students could show off their latest invention. Even though most students happily shared their discoveries, there were a few who liked to keep inventions under wraps until the big unveiling.

I was going to explain all this to Rowan, but when I turned around, he had disappeared again. Honestly, the kid needed a tracking device or something.

Luckily, I quickly caught sight of him this time. He was with a group on the other side of the shop. They stood behind a clear plastic panel and watched Mr. Adams give a demonstration using the company's hydraulic press. I joined them and smiled when I saw Rowan's eyes widen with amazement. Now he'd be ready if anyone ever asked him how much pressure it takes to crush a bowling ball. People get that question all the time, right?

Three hundred fifty kilonewtons, by the way.

There was a crackling sound overhead. "Attention,"

Mr. Brodigan's voice said from the building's PA system. "Is this on? Oh, okay." He cleared his throat. "Attention, everyone. The pizza's here! So make your way to the cafeteria. And security folks . . . come grab a couple of slices too. There's plenty for everyone."

We joined the herd of hungry kids as they made their way out of the shop and into the elevators. We rode up to the fourth floor and filed into the cafeteria with everyone else. The air was filled with the smell of every kind of pizza and the sound of excited students.

Rowan and I grabbed a couple of slices from the long table loaded with pizza boxes, and we snaked our way through the crowded hall to find my friends. We found Amy and Otis first.

"Hi, Amy! Hi, Otis!" Rowan said with his mouth full. He was already working on his second slice. He reached out and gently stroked the tiny Chihuahua's head. "Can he have some pizza?"

"Maybe just a *tiny* piece of cheese," Amy replied.

Rowan pulled off a small piece of cheese and held it out to Otis. The dog gave it a single sniff before snapping it up.

"How's your project going?" I asked.

"I printed most of the components," she replied. "I have to assemble them next." She scratched the dog behind the ears. "I'm going to start with Otis's cart."

"I bet he can't wait," I said.

Amy smiled. "Me either!" She glanced around. "Do you think I can take this pizza back with me?" she asked. "I want to hurry and get started."

I shrugged. "Sure, if you want." For all the times I've visited my dad's company, I didn't know them to have a food-in-the-cafeteria-only policy.

"Excellent idea," Sam said as she walked up with a paper plate of her own. She had her hair pulled into a ponytail and still wore her prescription sports goggles. "I'm so close to beating my top speed."

"Which is?" I asked.

"Forty-one KPH," she said proudly.

"Nice," I said, giving her a fist bump. I turned to see Rowan looking up at me, confused. "Around twenty-six miles per hour," I explained.

"Oh," said Rowan. "Do you think I can try out the skates on the track?"

Sam ruffled his hair. "Sure. You're a natural." She glanced at me and grinned.

"We'll come by later," said Rowan. "Tom's showing me the whole place!"

"Okay, see you then," said Sam. She and Amy pushed through the crowd toward the door.

"Was it something I said?" Noah asked as he walked up with his own plate. "Do I smell? I'm not the one doing time trials around the track all afternoon."

Sam shook her head and Amy waved him away as they disappeared into the crowd.

"Man, I may have to eat on the run too," Noah said between bites. "I'm not even halfway finished." He shook his head. "I can't believe this was my big lock-in project. It's starting to get boring, dude."

"I was going to ask how it was going, but . . ." Rowan pulled at my shirtsleeve.

"Can I get some more pizza?" he asked.

"You don't have to ask me," I said. "Have as much as you like."

"Thanks," Rowan said, and headed back toward the pizza table.

When he was far enough away, Noah elbowed my arm. "How's it going with you-know-who?"

"Not bad, actually," I replied. "He's a good kid."

I was surprised at how much fun I was having. It had been cool seeing everything through Rowan's eyes. I'd been there so many times that part of me forgot how amazing the place was.

"That's great," said Noah. "Because you should've seen your face when you walked into class with him this morning." He made an exaggerated frown. "You were all like, '*You guys go have fun, I'll just drag this kid around all day.*'"

"I didn't say that," I said. I couldn't help but laugh at his stretched face.

"It was in the eyes, dude," Noah said. "All in your eyes. They were saying . . ." He pouted his lips. "*I'm Tom Swift the inventor! Not Tom Swift the babysitter.*"

I laughed even harder. "Dude, that's not even . . ."

I stopped laughing when I spotted Rowan standing there, mouth open.

"Oh man," Noah whispered. "Rowan, I was just kidding around."

The boy spun around, tossed his plate onto a nearby table, and ran into the crowd.

"Rowan!" I shouted as I took off after him.

"Sorry," Noah called after us, but I didn't stop.

Rowan had a big head start. He was smaller and could zigzag through the pack much easier than I could. I just caught a glimpse of him as he exited the cafeteria and disappeared.

I finally made my way out of the crowd and into the hallway. I turned left and sprinted down the empty corridor. I hopped over a B-bot and turned the corner. Rowan was nowhere to be found. The only sign that anyone had come that way was the loud clack of a closing door. I ran to the door and flung it open. Rows of offices and cubicles spread out before me.

"Rowan?" I called as I stepped inside.

I moved deeper into the abandoned area and listened. The only sound was the door shutting behind me.

"Rowan?" I called again. "You in here?"

"I'm doing a job, you know," came his voice from the other end of the room. "I'm helping my dad. You're not babysitting me." He sounded as if he was ducked down behind one of the cubicles.

"Look, Noah was just joking," I explained. "He . . ."

"Warning. Warning." A woman's automated voice boomed through the PA system. "Quarantine lockdown in effect."

Rowan's head poked out from behind the last cubicle. "What's that mean?"

I glanced around. "I don't know." I had never heard that voice before.

"Quarantine lockdown in effect," the voice repeated.

CLACK!

The loud noise came from the entry. I ran back to it and tried the handle. It wouldn't budge. I jogged down the cubicle bay to the other exit. I grabbed the handle with both hands and tried to turn it. It wouldn't move no matter how hard I tried.

We were locked in.

7

The Adherence Disappearance

ROWAN RATTLED THE DOOR HANDLE AGAIN. "IT won't open," he repeated for the third time. Each was more frantic than the last.

"It'll be okay," I said. "I'm sure it won't be for long."

"How do you know?" he asked. "Does this happen a lot?"

"Well, no," I replied. "Not that I know of."

Honestly, I didn't even know the building could go into lockdown, much less a quarantine. I didn't even know that the company had any kind of contagious . . . anything. I knew my dad worked on some top secret stuff, but never anything like that. Now I was beginning to worry.

I went to the nearest cubicle and tried the phone. I pressed different line buttons and dialed zero but nothing happened. I tried the next cubicle—same thing.

That was strange. I got why all the doors had to be locked for a quarantine. If there was some kind of contamination, locking down all the office sections was the safest way to keep it from spreading. That didn't explain why the phones didn't work. You couldn't catch a disease through a phone line.

Rowan slid down the door and sat on the floor. He looked like he was close to tears. "I just want to go to my dad."

I knelt in front of him. "Don't be scared. We're safe in here." I pointed at the door. "And your dad's fine too. He's probably locked in with everyone else in the cafeteria." I gave a smile. "At least they have pizza."

"And you're stuck here babysitting me," Rowan said pointedly. His eyes blazed.

"Aw, come on. Noah was just joking," I explained. "And he was making fun of me, not you."

Rowan's lower lip trembled. "Then why were you laughing so much?"

I slid over to sit beside him. "Look, I'll admit that I wasn't expecting to have . . . a sidekick for this field trip. And that's what Noah was joking about." I shrugged. "But it turns out that you're a pretty cool guy. I'm having fun showing you around."

Rowan stood and wiped at an eye. I didn't think he believed me.

"What about that?" He pointed to an air vent high up on the wall. "We could get out that way."

"You watch way too many movies," I said. "Besides, if this is a real emergency, we need to stay put."

Rowan's shoulders drooped. "You're right. A place like this probably has laser beams or saw blades to keep people from sneaking through the air vents."

Wow. The kid *did* watch way too many movies.

"Look." I put a hand on his shoulder and led him toward one of the offices. "There'll probably be police cars outside already. Maybe even a couple of news vans."

Hey, what if Rowan's dad didn't write the story about me after all? The bigger story had to be the lockdown, right? I mean, I would hate it if one of the academy students accidentally broke a vial holding some dangerous disease. It seemed unlikely, but who knows what caused the alarm. Whatever happened, Mr. Kavner would have an inside exclusive. I was torn between worrying about the quarantine and being relieved that I may no longer be the focus of the story.

We entered the office and peered out the large window. Luckily, we faced the front of the building, the main entrance, the parking lot, and the academy across the street. Unluckily . . . the scene was dead outside. There were no cop cars, fire trucks, and not one news van.

"Where is everyone?" Rowan asked.

"I don't know," I said as I scanned the scene.

Then I spotted a pair of headlights moving down the street. "There!" I pointed. As the lights grew closer, I saw that they were indeed on a police car. "See? There you go."

"Just one car?" asked Rowan.

"They probably only send one out at first to see if it's a false alarm," I explained.

The cruiser slowed as it reached the main entrance. A spotlight burst from the car, aimed at the academy front doors.

"What are they doing?" Rowan asked.

I shook my head. "I don't know."

The spotlight shut off, and I sighed with relief as the cruiser turned into the Swift Enterprises parking lot. But then it stopped.

"What are you waiting for?" I asked, rubbing my hands together.

The police car backed out, merely using the parking lot entrance to turn around and face the way it had come. I frowned as the cruiser pulled away, headed up the dark street, and disappeared into the night.

"Hey!" Rowan shouted, waving his arms. "Over here!"

"They can't see or hear you," I said, knocking on the window. "The glass is reflective and too thick *and* we're too far away."

"Well shouldn't there be an alarm or something?" Rowan asked, panic rising in his voice. "If this were a real emergency, shouldn't the police know about it?"

"I would think so," I replied.

"But what if something's really wrong and *nobody* knows about it?" Rowan asked.

He had a point there. I wished I could call the police myself, or at least call my dad. The phone lines shouldn't be down for just that reason. I knocked on the glass window again. Then I got an idea. I dug my phone out of my pocket.

"I thought our phones wouldn't work," Rowan said.

"That's right," I said as I turned on my phone. Sure enough, no signal.

"Then what are we going to do?" asked Rowan. "We have to do something!" His voice rose in pitch and cracked, as if he was holding back tears.

"Here, help me move this desk over to the window," I said as I grabbed one side.

Rowan went to the other side and pushed as I pulled. When the desk was next to the window, I climbed on top of it. I faced the window and slid my phone back into my pocket. When I stretched my hand up toward the corner of the window, I could just barely reach it.

"Do you know what a Faraday cage is?" I asked, but I didn't give him a chance to answer. I had to keep his mind busy so he wouldn't start panicking. "No? Well, let me tell you. It was invented by Michael Faraday, and it's a wire cage that surrounds something and keeps electricity from getting through."

I scraped at the corner with my fingernail. "It can

also keep radio signals from getting through. Like cell signals."

My nail caught the edge of the invisible film covering the glass. "When they shield buildings like this, it's easy to put a metal cage or mesh in the walls," I continued as I began to pull at the thin film. "But the signal can still get through the windows. That's why they add this special film that blocks them."

I caught more of the film now. "So if I can pull away enough of this, I might be able to get a signal out."

I flicked the corner of the film with my finger some more until I finally got a grip. I pulled at it and it began to peel. I got about four centimeters free before it stopped. I pulled as hard as I could but I couldn't get any more to come off.

"Maybe this will be enough." I dug out my phone and held it up to the exposed corner. It was no good. I still didn't have a signal.

"Well, I thought it was a good plan," I said as I turned to face Rowan. I scanned the empty office. He was gone again.

Like I said, tracking device.

"Rowan?" I called as I hopped off the desk.

I left the office and scanned the large cubicle bay, but he was nowhere to be found. I ran to the exit and tried the handle. It was still locked. He hadn't gotten out that way.

I was about to start checking cubicles, when I spotted the desk pushed up against the far wall. A stool stood atop the desk along with the faceplate from the air vent. There was also a letter opener on the desk next to a couple of screws.

He didn't.

I jumped onto the desk and climbed on top of the stool. I stuck my head into the opening. "Rowan?"

There was no answer.

"Rowan! Come back here!" Still no answer. "What about the laser beams, Rowan?"

Nothing.

8

The Constrained Estrangement

I COULDN'T BELIEVE I WAS DOING THIS. I WAS crawling, Bruce Willis style, through the air vents of my dad's company. It was cramped, dark, and, worst of all, very, very cold. They don't tell you about that in movies, do they? They're called air vents because, you know, air blows through them—cold air, as in air-conditioning. If it wasn't so dark I bet I would've been able to see my breath. As it was, I could barely make out the thin metal surface around me.

"Rowan!" I shouted. My voice echoed down the shaft ahead of me.

Again there was no reply.

I crawled farther, toward a dim light ahead. As it got closer, I saw that it was another slatted vent cover. I reached it and peeked out through the slats to see another set of offices and cubicles. The cover was still attached, so I know he hadn't gotten out there.

And come to think of it, how was he supposed to get out once he found a vent leading to where he wanted to go? He had unscrewed the first cover from the *outside*. You couldn't do it from the inside. Did he even have a plan for getting out? Maybe the kid was more like me than I'd thought—act first and plan later.

I crawled farther along, the only light coming from the occasional vent cover I passed. I soon entered a stretch where there were no vent covers at all. Even as my eyes adjusted to the dim light, there were no more outlets along the way. Soon, I was in total darkness.

I tried to remain calm as I felt my way along. It was cold, pitch-black, and very cramped. I'd never been claustrophobic before, but with my shoulders sliding along the sides as I moved and having to keep my head down to avoid bumping it, I was beginning to see why some people were.

"Rowan?" I called again. This time I heard a little shakiness in my voice.

Suddenly, the pressure was gone from my shoulders. I stopped and felt around. I was in the middle of a four-way junction. Which way could he have gone? It was too dark to spot any clues.

"Rowan!" I shouted. "Come on, answer me!"

I listened for a reply, but none came.

I relaxed and tried to think. Which direction would he have chosen? He wanted to get to his dad. And Mr. Kavner was locked in the cafeteria along with everyone else. Now, in what direction would the cafeteria be from here? I backed up and took the shaft on the left.

I crawled through more frigid darkness with no light at the end of the tunnel, so to speak. It seemed weird that there was such a long stretch of venting without output to any more offices or hallways.

That wasn't the only weird thing. I slowly got the sensation that the shaft was sloping downward. The farther I crawled, the steeper the incline became. Soon, I had to push back with my hands as I crawled just to keep from sliding down. Now I was doing more pushing than crawling.

Okay, it was official. This was a bad idea. I could've done a *little* more planning before I acted this time.

I tried to back out the way I had come. I placed my hands on either side of the wall and pushed myself backward. My legs flailed as I strained to go in reverse. It was no use. The incline was too steep. I had no choice; I had to move ahead.

Keeping my palms planted on the walls, I let gravity take over. I slid forward, slowly at first. Then the slope increased and it was all I could do to hold myself back. My hands squeaked against the walls as I tried to keep myself from going faster.

Suddenly, my right hand came off the wall and I slammed forward. "Ahhh!" I shouted as I slid down with nothing to slow me. I covered my head with both arms and closed my eyes as I picked up speed.

My heart raced as I sped down the shaft like I was on a slide in a water park. Except there was no water, I could barely see anything, and I had no idea where I was going.

Finally, I slowed as the vent shaft leveled out. I squeaked as I slid to a stop.

"Tom?"

"Ah!" Startled, my head shot up and slammed against the top of the shaft.

I opened my eyes and could make out Rowan in the shaft ahead of me. He was a couple of meters away and his face was lit from below.

"Are you okay?" he asked me.

"I'm trapped in an air vent chasing after you," I replied, crawling toward him. "No, I'm not okay."

He pointed to the bottom of the shaft, the source of the light. "We're not trapped. Look."

I crawled closer and saw that a large vent cover was attached to the floor of the shaft in front of him. I peered through the slats and saw several white lines painted on the black floor below. Suddenly, someone sped through the scene. It was Sam. We were above the testing track.

"Sam!" I shouted.

"Sam! Up here!" Rowan added.

I waited to see her come back into view, but she never did.

That was weird. The ceiling above the track wasn't so high. She should've been able to hear us. I craned my neck, trying to see where she'd gone, but we must have been positioned near the far wall of the huge room. I could only make out a small section of track.

"Could you see her from your side?" I asked Rowan.

"For a while," he replied. "But she kept skating."

I looked up at Rowan. We were face-to-face above the vent cover.

"Hey, how did you turn around?" I asked him. He was smaller than me, but not small enough to easily spin around in the cramped shaft.

Rowan jutted a thumb over his shoulder. "There's a four-way split back there."

Huh. It didn't even occur to me that I could use the split to turn around. Smart kid. I craned my neck to see through the vent slats again. I could barely see any of the room below.

"Back up past the junction," I said. "I want to turn around to get a better look."

"Okay," Rowan replied as he shimmied backward.

Once he was clear of the cover, I began to crawl over it. I was almost across when I realized I had made a serious miscalculation—I weighed a lot more than Rowan did.

The vent cover fell away beneath me. My stomach sank and my arms flailed as I tried to grab on to something. My hands quickly found the edge of the dangling cover. Luckily, one side of the cover was hinged to the overhead vent. Still, my hands slid down the sides as momentum carried me downward. I grunted as I clamped on to the cover as hard as I could. My hands stopped sliding and my body slowly swung to a stop as I dangled over the track below.

My feet were only a meter over the floor, but I held on a moment to catch my breath. I turned my head and saw Sam barreling toward me. She was watching the track and not what was hanging above it.

"Sam!" I shouted. She was so close that I didn't have enough time to drop and roll out of the way. "Sam!"

Finally, she glanced up and her eyes widened. She folded into a crouch as I lifted my legs as high as I could. She sped safely beneath me.

She slowed to a stop as I dropped onto the track.

"What in the world are you doing?" she asked, skating back to me.

"Well," I began, still catching my breath. "Funniest thing . . ."

"Hang on," she said. Then she reached up and removed the wireless earbuds from her ears.

"That's why you didn't answer us," I said.

"Us?" she asked.

I looked up and Sam followed my gaze. Rowan's head appeared through the opening in the air vent. He gave a small wave.

"Okay." Sam put her hands on her hips. "What are you two up to?"

I pointed up at Rowan. "Someone didn't like being locked up," I explained. "He got a little creative with his escape plan."

"Locked up?" asked Sam. "Why was he locked up?" She cut me a harsh look. "What did you do to him, Swift?"

I raised my hands. "Hey, I didn't do anything. I'm talking about the quarantine."

Sam shook her head. "What quarantine?"

No wonder we found Sam skating around the track like nothing happened. She was listening to music and didn't hear the announcement. I quickly explained about the quarantine lockdown and how the authorities didn't seem to know about it.

Sam's eyes widened. "Do you think there's some kind of contagious disease outbreak?"

I shook my head. "I don't think my dad works with anything like that."

"Some kind of chemical spill?" Sam suggested. "Why else would the building even be set up for a quarantine?"

I shrugged. "I don't know."

She glanced at the doors on the other side of the track. "No wonder no one came back from the cafeteria."

The testing track and gym took up most of the second floor. And thanks to the lockdown, we seemed to have the whole floor to ourselves.

"Uh . . ." Rowan said from above. "Do you think there's a ladder around or something?"

Sam pulled off her skates and ran toward the end of the track. "Give me a hand," she said. "I have an idea."

I followed her to the wall end of the track, toward the pads that lined it. The pads were a safety feature lining the wall in case someone or something lost control on a turn. Sam reached up and pulled at a large pad attached to the wall. The Velcro fasteners made a ripping sound as the pad detached. I did the same with the pad next to it. After we made two more trips, they were soon in a stack almost as tall as me and directly under Rowan.

"All right," Sam said to Rowan. "Slide your feet out and then just drop down."

"Are you sure?" Rowan asked nervously.

"You got this," I called up to him. Then I turned to Sam. "He does, doesn't he?"

Sam waved me away. "It'll be easy," she told him.

Rowan dangled his feet out of the opening. He then took a deep breath and pushed off. He plopped onto the pads, which slowly compressed with a loud hiss. Sam and I helped him down.

"Okay, now what?" asked Rowan.

"Did you try calling security?" Sam asked.

"We were stuck in some offices," I replied. "None of the phones worked."

Sam pointed to the other side of the track. "Let's try that one."

We ran across the track to the abandoned security desk beside the glass entry doors. The guard that was supposed to be posted there was probably in the cafeteria with everyone else.

Sam picked up the receiver and held it to her ear. She pressed a few buttons and listened again. "This one's dead too."

"Hey, look!" Rowan pointed to the computer monitor at the desk. A small window showed black-and-white footage from one of the security cameras. The image cycled from one empty hallway to another and then to an empty office space.

"Think we can bring up a camera from the cafeteria?" asked Sam.

I sat down at the security desk and moved the mouse. After some trial and error, I finally clicked on the correct icon. Rows of thumbnail images filled the screen. I clicked on one labeled CAF_001.

Footage from the cafeteria security camera filled the screen. Just as we thought, most of our group were still there. Some kids milled around, while others sat at tables. A group of adults stood talking way in the background.

"Is there a camera near them?" Rowan asked, pointing at the group of adults.

I cycled through the other cameras until I found one that showed a closer view of the adults.

"Where's my dad?" Rowan asked.

I scanned the people in the shot. "I don't see him."

Sam put a hand on Rowan's shoulder. "I'm sure he's fine. These cameras can't catch everyone."

Rowan pointed to the group of thumbnails. "Can you try a camera somewhere else?"

"Sure." I moved the curser to the thumbnails and selected six of them. When I clicked the selection, six video feeds filled the screen. But even though they were video feeds, they looked like static images. The hallways, labs, and office spaces were empty, so there was nothing moving.

"What's that?" asked Sam. She pointed to the top right corner of one of the feeds. There was a bit of movement in the monitored hallway.

I leaned in for a closer look. "Someone's there, all right." I could make out a pair of legs at the end of an empty corridor, but the rest of the person was just out of frame. The person seemed to be pacing, and I couldn't tell if it was a man or woman, adult or student.

"Who is that?" Sam asked.

"Look," said Rowan.

The mystery person stopped pacing and began walking toward the camera. Then the screen became gray static.

"What happened?" asked Sam.

"I don't know," I replied. I closed the window and

relaunched it. Still static. Then another one of the six screens became static. And then another.

Then the really freaky thing happened: The first screen cleared. There was no static and there was no longer anyone in frame. A fourth screen went to static as the second frame cleared. It was as if the static intentionally masked the identity of the person walking past them.

"Someone's bypassing the cameras," Sam muttered.

"What does that mean?" asked Rowan.

I stared at the screens. More went to static as more cleared. "It means this quarantine lockdown may not be real after all."

The Distraction Infraction

"WE'VE BEEN LOCKED UP FOR NO REASON?!"
Rowan exclaimed.

"Maybe. I don't know," I said as I scanned through the other video feeds. "Hang on a second, I need to think."

I had lost the trail of bypassed security feeds. The last static screen I spotted was on the fourth floor somewhere. Whoever was moving through the company had either stopped or moved to an area I hadn't found yet.

I knew Swift Enterprises worked on all kinds of top secret projects. But I couldn't believe someone would lock down the entire building just to steal one. Then again, what other reason could it be? We had to report what we knew before they had time to finish their heist.

"Tom, we have to tell someone," Sam said, as if reading my mind.

"How?" asked Rowan. "None of the phones work."

"And who would we tell?" I asked. "If someone can bypass the security feeds so easily, it might be one of the security guards."

"It can't be all of them," Sam said. "We should tell as many of them as we can."

That was a good plan. There was just one problem. "How do we get to them?" I asked. "We're still on lock-down."

"We'll find a way," Sam said. "You guys got in here, right?"

Rowan shook his head. "I don't want to go back into the vents."

"Don't worry," I said. "We'd need a ladder to get up to it at this point. Besides, we're lucky we got this far. It's a maze up there."

Rowan shivered. "And very cold."

"Fine," Sam said. "Any other ideas?"

Rowan glanced at the glass entry doors and then back to the security desk. "When we were in the first room, you know, to make your circuit boards, the guard hit a button under his desk to unlock the doors."

I shook my head. "I don't know if it's going to be that easy—"

BUZZZZ-KLAK!

Sam had reached under the desk and found the button. Rowan ran over to the double doors and pushed one. It swung open.

Sam and I looked at each other, and I shrugged. Then I followed her as we ran through the open door. We entered the smaller area with the gym entrance, the elevator, and stair access. Rowan released the door and it slowly swung back into place.

"Wait!" I dove for the door and caught it just before it shut. "We should prop this open," I suggested. "It'll probably lock again, and we'll be trapped in here if we don't find a way out."

"Good idea." Sam ran back into the track room and grabbed the security guard's chair. She rolled it into place, blocking the door from shutting all the way.

I ran to the stairs and tried the access door. It was

locked. Sam tried the gym door while Rowan pressed the call button on the elevator. All three were dead ends.

"It was worth a shot," Sam said.

Rowan left the call button alone and moved to the elevator doors. He jammed his fingers into the gap between the doors and tried to force them open.

"Dude, again, way too many movies," I said.

Sam shrugged. "Any better ideas?"

Fair point. I shook my head. "No, not really."

Sam and I moved to the elevator doors and added our strength to Rowan's. Even with Sam pulling one door, Rowan pulling the other, and me trying to pry open both, we barely got them five centimeters apart. We all grunted as we finally gave up.

"We need some leverage," Sam suggested. "Something to pry with."

"Got a crowbar handy?" I joked.

Sam got that look in her eyes—the look that means she's getting an idea and is about to do or say something totally insane. "Hold that thought."

She ran back into the track room. Rowan and I watched as she darted across the track.

"You think she might have a crowbar in there?" I asked him.

Rowan shrugged.

Sam ran back with what looked like an old mic stand. It was a silver pipe on a round black base.

"What's that?" asked Rowan.

"The stand for the motion-activated camera," she explained. "It's like the one they use for photo finishes in horse races. That's how I accurately tested my speed."

This time, Rowan and I each grabbed a door and pulled. When the gap was big enough, Sam jammed the end of the stand inside. She wrenched it to one side and the gap opened wider. She grunted as she pulled the rod harder. Then something gave and the doors opened completely.

I put an arm out to keep Rowan from falling into the open shaft, but it turned out that I didn't have to worry. The elevator was parked on the floor below us, and its top was level with our floor.

Sam jammed the stand into the opening to keep the doors from closing again. "Okay, now what?" she asked.

Rowan peered down at the elevator. "Is there a hatch on the roof? Maybe we can climb into the elevator and get out on the floor below us."

"Then we'll have two sets of doors to pry open," Sam said. "And in a cramped area."

I pulled out my phone and activated the flashlight app. The bright white screen appeared and I held it into the shaft. It illuminated the cables, the side of the shaft, and the service ladder stretching up the side.

"Check it out," I said, pointing to the ladder. I followed it up and spotted a small hatch on the floor above.

"Where does that go?" Sam asked.

"Let's find out," I said as I stepped onto the elevator roof.

"What if the elevator goes to the top floor?" Rowan asked. "You'll be crushed."

I carefully stepped around the cables and toward the ladder. "If the doors are on lockdown, the elevators will be too," I said.

I climbed up the ladder toward the small hatch. When I was level with it, I reached out and grabbed the handle. I had a feeling that it would be locked tight and we would be no better off than when we started. I gave it a turn and heard the lock disengage. The small door swung inward.

"Cool!" said Rowan. He began to step onto the elevator.

"Hang on a minute," I said, digging out my phone again. I wanted to make sure this wasn't a dead end.

It turned out that I didn't need a flashlight. The narrow corridor beyond was lit by intermittent lights near the floor. Spaced on either side of the plain walls, they stretched all the way down the tunnel. The ceiling was the same height as a regular hallway but was crowded with pipes and electrical conduits. I was in some sort of building maintenance corridor.

"Well?" asked Sam.

"I don't know where it goes," I called down. "But it's a way out of here."

Apparently, that's all Rowan needed to hear. He stepped onto the elevator and moved to the ladder. He quickly scaled the distance and I stepped through the hatch to give him room to enter.

As Sam followed Rowan up the ladder, the elevator shaft filled with a loud hum.

The elevator began to rise.

10

The Convergence Occurrence

ROWAN SCRAMBLED INTO THE HATCH AND crawled into the corridor. Once he was clear, I leaned out to check on Sam. She hurried up the ladder, but the elevator was coming up fast.

"Come on!" I shouted. I leaned down and reached out for her.

When she was close enough, I grabbed her arm. I held tight and flung myself backward. Sam flew through the hatch just as the elevator whizzed by. We landed in a heap on the corridor floor.

Sam pushed herself up. "Thanks," she said as she got

to her feet. Then she extended a hand and helped me to mine. When we were both standing, she gave my shoulder a hard shove. "I thought you said the elevators were locked down!"

I raised my hands in defense. "How would I know? This is my first lockdown too, you know."

I poked my head out of the open hatch and watched the elevator continue up the dark shaft. It was too dark to see where it stopped.

"Do you think whoever bypassed the camera can override the elevator somehow?" Sam asked.

"Seems like it," I replied. "I wish I could see what floor it stopped on." Whoever was inside was one step closer to their goal, and we were still no closer to reporting what we knew. I thought about climbing the ladder after the elevator. But if it descended, I'd be toast.

"Hey, check it out!" came Rowan's voice, way too far away. The kid had run off again.

Sam and I moved down the narrow hallway until we turned a corner. We came around and saw Rowan staring at the ground next to several arched openings along one wall. Several B-bots were parked against the other wall. Most of them had tiny blinking red lights on them. Some of them had solid green lights.

"Wow, so this is where they go," said Sam.

A B-bot appeared through one of the small arches and rolled to a stop over a large rectangle on the floor. I could just make out the rectangle falling away under the robot. A motor whirred before dust and small bits of trash fell out of the robot and into the opening.

"Cool," said Rowan.

The trap door closed and the robot continued forward. It then stopped, turned, and backed against the wall like the others. It locked into a small charging station and its own red light began to blink. Immediately, one of the green light B-bots rolled away from the wall and exited through the nearest archway.

"So now what?" asked Sam.

I studied our surroundings. The tunnel went on for another few meters before turning another corner. Then I spotted something just before the turn.

"Check it out," I said, running down the corridor. I was careful not to kick any of the charging B-bots. I stopped at a ladder leading up to an opening in the ceiling, and I saw a similar environment through the open hatch above. The ladder must lead to the maintenance corridor on the next floor up.

"These B-bots are all over the company, right?" I asked.

"Yeah?" asked Sam.

I pointed to the ladder. "So there must be tunnels like this throughout the entire facility. I bet they'll take us anywhere we want to go."

"That's great," Sam said. "But how do we get out of this tunnel once we get there?"

Rowan knelt on the ground and poked his head out of one of the arches. "I bet I can fit through. . . ." He gasped and pulled away from the opening. He looked up at us with wide eyes. "There's someone out there," he whispered.

I knelt too and eased toward the opening. I spotted someone slowly moving down the main hallway. From the low angle, I could see their sneakers and the bottom of their jeans.

"Who is it?" Sam asked.

The feet stopped, as if the owner had heard Sam's question. I pulled away from the wall and made a shushing gesture to Sam and Rowan. Then I eased back toward the opening. I came face-to-face with . . .

"Ah!" Noah shouted.

"Ah!" I echoed.

"Dude, is Sam all right?" my best friend asked.

"Her?!" I barked. "*I'm* the one you just scared half to death!"

"I'm here, Noah," Sam said.

Noah sighed with relief. "Oh, good. I thought that elevator squished you."

I shook my head. "How did you know about that?"

Noah sat down cross-legged. "I've been locked in this hallway the whole time. There was nothing to do but watch everyone on the security feed." He laughed. "I lost you and Rowan for a long time after you went all Bruce Willis through the air vents."

I smirked. "I'm glad we could keep you entertained."

"How did you know where to find us?" asked Sam.

"It was hard to see clearly, but I saw you climb into the service hatch in the elevator shaft," Noah replied.

"Any idea how we get out of here?" I asked.

Noah shrugged. "There's got to be an exit around there somewhere," he explained. "People have to get in there to service stuff, right? It can't be convenient to climb over the elevator every time."

He had a point. I stood and moved down the tunnel, scanning the walls. Sure enough, I spotted a door with one of those push-latches across its middle, like an emergency exit door.

"Found it!" I shouted. I pushed the bar and the door swung open.

Noah was there waiting on the other side. "Cool! You can't even tell there's a door from this side."

Sam and Rowan followed me out. I heard the door hissing shut behind them and I thought of the chair propping open the test track door.

"Wait!" I said, lurching for it. "Don't let it . . ."

The door clicked shut and I saw that Noah was right. You couldn't tell there was a door there.

"Now we're trapped," I said.

"I can get it," Rowan announced. He got down on the ground and shimmied through the nearest archway. A second later, the door was open again.

"That's good to know," said Sam.

Noah grabbed the open door. "Cool, let's get out of here."

"Wait a minute," I told him. "You said you were watching the security feeds?"

Noah pointed down the corridor. "Yeah, from the security station. The guy never came back."

"Can you show us?" I asked.

While we followed Noah down the hall, we filled him in on the static we'd seen at our security station.

"Yeah, I saw a couple like that," Noah said. "I just thought the cameras were down."

"When we saw them," Sam added, "the cameras were down in a pattern, like they were hiding someone traveling though the halls."

"So this 'quarantine' may be a fake?" Noah asked.

"I don't know," I said. "But if someone's using the lockdown to steal from the company, then we're the only ones who know about it."

We reached the security desk and Noah plopped down in the chair. After a few keystrokes and some quick mousework, he had pulled up the same selection of thumbnails I had found.

Noah leaned back in the chair. "All right, what am I looking for?"

"Look for any camera feeds that are just static," Sam suggested.

"I don't think you know what you're asking," Noah

said as he scrolled through the long group of thumbnails. There must have been hundreds of security cameras in the building.

My heart sank. It would take forever to scan through each of those feeds.

"Is there any way to just search the cameras in high-security areas?" Sam asked.

"Good idea," Noah said as he began to type. "Security has these cameras tagged and cross-referenced in tons of different ways."

"How do you know that?" I asked.

Noah grinned up at me. "I told you I had some time on my hands."

It wasn't long before Noah had the list narrowed down to around twenty thumbnails. He began cycling through them. I recognized a couple of the chemical labs, the engineering section, an electronics lab, and then the screen went to static.

"Where's that?" asked Sam.

Noah highlighted the thumbnail. It was labeled SERVER_011_MAIN. "I think that's the server room."

"Can you check the other cameras in there?" I asked.

Noah's fingers raced over the keyboard, and ten

more thumbnails appeared. He quickly cycled through them, and every one of them showed nothing but static.

"All the cameras in there are offline," Noah said.

"Then that's where they are," I said.

"Where is it located?" Sam asked me. Rowan looked up at me as well.

I shrugged. "I don't know. Just because it's my dad's company doesn't mean I have the place memorized."

Noah pulled out his phone. "Luckily I do." He opened his new mapping app. "Or at least my phone does."

"Did you finish mapping the entire facility?" I asked.

"Just about," Noah said as he swiped through some screens on his phone. "Here it is. Fifth floor."

"Think you can get us there through the maintenance tunnels?" I asked him.

Noah got to his feet. "I can get us close, at least." He pulled out his phone and tapped the screen. "If the tunnels generally run parallel with the main hallways on every floor . . ." He tapped his screen again. "Then I should be able to add them to the map I've already built."

Rowan pointed to the security station computer.

"Can't you just unlock everything?" he asked. "End the quarantine?"

Noah smiled and raised his hands. "Not that I *tried* something like that. But if I had, then I might've figured out that it can only be done from the main security console. Not one like this."

I laughed. "Not that you would've tried anything like that."

Noah shook his head vigorously. "Oh, no."

Sam rolled her eyes.

Noah led the way as we jogged down the corridors. After a couple of turns, Noah checked his app again and looked up. "Okay, the entrance is right around here, two floors above us."

I turned to Rowan. "All right. You're up."

Rowan grinned and darted to the nearest B-bot hole. He crawled through and disappeared inside. The three of us glanced around, wondering where the hidden door would be.

When I was little, my mom and dad used to read me stories about castles full of hidden passageways and secret rooms. I wonder if my dad had any of that in mind when he helped design this place.

It seemed as if Rowan was gone for too long. I began to wonder if he had run off again when part of the wall swung open a few meters away.

"Sorry," he said. "I had trouble finding this one."

"No problem," I said. "And great job."

He held the door open as Sam and I followed Noah inside. When the door clicked shut behind us, Noah checked his phone and headed back in the direction where we had been waiting and searched for an access ladder. Luckily, we found one nearby, and climbed up to the next level.

When we reached the next floor, everyone scanned the area for another ladder. They seemed to be staggered on each floor, so there wasn't one in plain sight. We carefully stepped over parked B-bots while looking for the next one. Noah kept his eyes on the map, keeping track of how far we strayed from our objective.

Just then a growl echoed through the thin passage.

"What was that?" Sam whispered.

"Sounds like an animal," I replied.

"Does your dad do animal experiments?" asked Rowan.

"No way," I replied.

The growl grew louder.

"Look," Noah whispered. He pointed to a nearby corner.

The shape of an animal was projected on the opposite wall. It bared sharp teeth as the shadow grew larger.

The Abduction Deduction

"WHAT IS THAT?" ROWAN ASKED AS HE SIDE-
stepped behind me.

The growling grew louder and then something darted
around the corner. I stopped short, confused, when one
of the B-bots wheeled into view. Was something wrong
with its motor? And what had made the shadow?

Then something else tore around the corner. It was
Otis! The little Chihuahua ran after the robot, teeth
bared, with a low growl rising from his throat. The little
dog's back legs were suspended off the ground as his
back end rode inside a bright green cart.

"Otis!" Rowan shouted as he moved ahead of me.

The Chihuahua skidded to a stop and cocked his head. Then he panted and ran toward Rowan, the B-bot all but forgotten. His cart's wheels whirred behind him.

Rowan knelt and stroked the excited dog. "Amy fixed you up good, huh, boy?"

"How did he get here?" asked Sam.

"Otis!" called Amy's distant voice.

Sam, Noah, and I looked at one another. Then we scooted past Rowan and Otis and ran down the tiny corridor. We rounded the corner and spotted Amy's head poking through one of the robot holes. When she saw us, she squeaked in surprise and ducked out of sight.

"Amy!" Sam shouted. "It's okay, it's us."

We crouched around the opening and Amy slowly poked her head back through. "How did you get in there?" she asked. Then her eyes widened. "Did you see Otis?"

"Yeah, he's with Rowan," Noah replied.

"Rowan's in there too?"

I stood and glanced around. Luckily, one of the access doors was nearby. I pushed it open and found myself in the 3-D printing lab. Amy got to her feet when Sam and Noah followed me out. Noah grabbed a nearby stool and propped open the door.

Usually, Amy didn't have a hair out of place or a wrinkled garment in sight. Now, however, her hair was frizzed while her face and clothes were covered with dirt.

"What happed to you?" I asked. "Are you all right?"

Amy tightened her lips as she tried to smooth down her hair. "Oh . . . Otis had been giving those robots the stink eye all day," she explained. "And when I finally finished his cart and got him all set up, was he grateful?" She threw her hands up. "No! The first thing he did was go after one. He chased it into the wall and wouldn't come back no matter how much I called him." She shook her head. "I tried to go in after him . . ." Then she let out a long breath. "I didn't fit."

Amy must have been really upset. That's the most she had ever blurted out at once.

Amy opened her mouth to continue and then stopped. She squinted at us. "What were you doing in there?"

We quickly explained our theory of the fake lockdown, how we found the access tunnels, and where we were headed.

Amy pointed to the robot hole in the wall. "But if you can go anywhere you want now, shouldn't you go to the cafeteria and warn someone?"

"We will," I said. "But I want to go up to the server room to be sure."

"Otherwise the quarantine is real, and we might be spreading some kind of virus to everyone else," Noah said with a chuckle.

Amy's eyes darted between the three of us before slowly pulling her shirt collar over her mouth and nose.

"Otis seems so happy," Rowan said as he stepped out of the access tunnel. Otis panted as he proudly trotted out behind the boy. "Good job, Amy."

Amy knelt and scratched the little dog behind the ears. "I still have some adjustments to make."

I anxiously glanced at the open doorway. Who knew how long we'd have to find out who was in the server room?

"What do you think, Amy?" I asked. "You in?"

My shyest friend, who always followed the rules and tried her best to not draw attention to herself, gave a devious grin and nodded. "Oh yeah."

Amy gently unstrapped Otis from his new cart and

placed him back into his carrying pouch. Once the pouch was secure, she strapped the little cart to one of her belt loops and followed us into the tunnel.

Noah led the way with his app and quickly spotted another access ladder. When we reached the next level, the temperature was considerably cooler. As Noah then led us around another corner, the white noise of cooling fans grew louder and the temperature dropped.

Noah checked his phone and then pointed to the wall on our left. "This should be the server room."

"That's why it's so cold?" Sam remarked.

All the spinning hard drives in one room generated a lot of heat. Lots of places had entire air-conditioning systems dedicated to keeping them cool. Swift Enterprises seemed to be no exception. Thanks to a mishap with a missing drone, Noah and I knew firsthand that the academy used a similar system.

"Look," Amy said, pointing to the bottom of the wall.

Another B-bot rolled through another access hatch that had clear plastic strips hanging over it. The strips helped keep most of the cool air in the server room while letting the robots easily push through.

The robot pulled to a stop over this area's trash chute,

and the trapdoor fell away just before the robot dumped its payload.

But this time, there was a sound of something big and heavy going down the chute. It clanked and thudded, bouncing off the sides as it went down. My friends and I glanced at one another.

"What was that?" asked Sam.

"Sounded big," said Noah.

The robot left the chute and parked at a nearby charging station. As soon as its red light appeared, another B-bot pulled away from the wall. It rolled into the server room through another hatch, easily pushing through the plastic flaps.

I got to the floor and peered through the tiny doorway. Noah crawled over and stuck his head next to mine. Sam, Rowan, and Amy crouched near another doorway.

"I can't see anyone," he said.

"Me either," I agreed.

All I could see were the seemingly endless racks of hard drives. An organized web of cables attached them to each other. The many cooling fans going at once made it impossible to hear footsteps of any kind. But I did hear something else.

"Is that whistling?" whispered Noah.

"Yeah," I replied. Someone was in the server room, all right. And he or she was whistling.

Then I caught some movement. A shadow moved between two of the server racks. The glimpse was so brief that I couldn't make out any of the person's features. And even though the plastic flaps on the robot ports were clear, they were scuffed and cloudy, making it even harder to catch any detail.

Suddenly something blocked my view.

"Uh-oh, look out," I said, pulling my face away from the opening.

Noah and I had barely kept from being rammed by one of the B-bots. It trundled through and headed for the trash chute.

"Grab it," Noah ordered.

I had the exact same idea. My hands were already on it, and I lifted it off the ground. Its wheels spun helplessly.

"What are you doing?" Sam asked.

I flipped the robot onto its back. "Let's see what these things are dumping."

The robot had a curved suction vent near its front and two large doors covering most of its middle. They looked like mini bomb-bay doors, hinged on the outside with a slit down the middle. I tried to pry them open but I couldn't get any leverage.

I looked up at the others. "Does anybody have a—"

Before I could finish the question, Amy knelt beside me and reached into Otis's pouch. "Excuse me, Otis," she said as she pulled out what looked like a rolled-up piece of black canvas. She untied a cord and unrolled the cloth on the floor. Several thin pockets were sewn into the canvas, and each held a small tool.

Amy fished out a screwdriver and jammed it between the doors. After some effort, they snapped open to reveal an odd-shaped package inside.

"What is it?" asked Rowan.

I removed the package and turned it over in my hands. It was something wrapped tight in Bubble Wrap and clear packing tape.

"I don't suppose you have a knife in . . ."

Amy already had a craft knife removed from the tool pouch and held it out to me, handle first.

I took the knife and gently slit the packing tape. Then I unrolled the Bubble Wrap to reveal a thick gray box about the size of a large phone.

Noah gasped. "Dude, that's a hard drive," he said. "Someone's stealing data from your dad's company."

A knot tightened in my stomach. Not only had someone faked a quarantine, but that same person was using the distraction to steal from my father. There was no telling what kind of secrets were on this drive.

"Stealing?" asked Rowan. He pointed to the trash chute. "Aren't they just getting thrown away?"

"Exactly," said Sam. "Why smuggle these through security when you can pick them out of the trash later?"

Rowan's eyes widened. "Whoa."

A familiar clunking sound got everyone's attention. We turned to see that another B-bot had just dropped its payload into the garbage chute. And from the sound of it going down, it was yet another hard drive.

"We have to tell someone," Amy said.

Of course I didn't know *every* person in my father's company, but I knew a lot of them. Most were friendly, cheerful people who seemed to truly enjoy their jobs. From what I had heard over the years, Swift Enterprises was a cool company to work for. Everyone thought my dad was a great boss who treated people fairly. I couldn't believe one of his employees would betray him like that. I felt my mouth harden as I shook my head in disgust.

I handed Amy the hard drive. "Hold this, will you?" Then I crawled back to the robot hatch, but I still only caught movement near the bottom of the server racks.

I turned to my friends, who were already back at their own openings. "Can anyone see who's in there?"

Sam and Amy shook their heads. "The angle is too low," Sam said.

"I'll find out," said Rowan. He climbed toward the hatch and shimmied through before I realized what he was talking about.

"Rowan, no!" I said to him. But by that time, I was just talking to his sneakers. Then they, too, disappeared into the server room.

Sam and Amy crowded around one hatch while Noah and I looked through the other. From our angle, we could see Rowan crawling along one of the outside racks, and we could still hear the faint whistling, so we knew his cover wasn't blown. Then Rowan turned a corner and scrambled out of sight between the racks.

"That kid's crazy," I said, shaking my head.

"Hmm . . . he acts first and thinks later," Noah added. "Remind you of anyone?"

I cut Noah a quick glare before shuffling over to Sam and Amy. "Can you see him?" I asked.

"Not anymore," said Amy.

I could still hear the whistling amid the steady roar of the fans.

"I see movement," Sam reported. "But I can't tell if it's Rowan or not."

"Oh, yeah," Amy pointed. "Over there . . . nope. It's gone."

I couldn't stand to watch anymore, so I paced nervously behind them. What if this thief was violent? What if Rowan was discovered and the thief didn't want any witnesses?

Suddenly the flaps flew up from one of the openings and we all jumped with a start. Then Rowan grinned as he poked his head through. "I saw him," he announced as he began to shimmy back in.

We ran over and gathered around him.

"Okay, it's a him," Noah said, crouching beside the opening. "Did you recognize him?"

"No," Rowan replied.

Then the whistling stopped.

Sam cocked her head. "Uh, guys . . ."

"It's okay," Rowan said. "I can go back and . . ." His eyes widened and his arms flailed as he was jerked back into the server room.

12

The Observation Complication

I DOVE FOR THE OPENING AND JUST CAUGHT Rowan's hand before it disappeared. Noah reached in and grabbed the other one. We pulled until Rowan's face was through the opening again.

"He's got me! He's got me!" Rowan shouted.

Sam and Amy crowded in and grabbed on to his arms as well. Otis barked and Rowan yelled as we played tug-of-war with whoever was on the other side of the wall.

When more of Rowan had been pulled through, I reached down and grabbed his belt. I placed my feet against the wall to get more leverage. I grunted as I pushed with my legs and pulled with my arms. Once Noah got into a similar position, we made better progress. With all four of us pulling, Rowan finally came all the way through. We landed in a heap against the opposite wall.

"Are you okay?" Amy asked Rowan as we scrambled to our feet.

He shivered and his lower lip trembled. "I . . . I just want my dad."

"Okay, let's get out of here!" I said. I didn't know if the thief knew how to get into the service tunnel, so I wanted to put as much distance between him and us as possible.

I led the way as we took off down the narrow corridor. I hopped over a robot, darted around the corner, and hit the access ladder, practically sliding down it to the floor below.

Once everyone was down the ladder, we stopped panting. "Can you find the shortest route to the cafeteria?" I asked Noah.

"Working on it," Noah replied as he swiped at his phone. He led the way down the narrow tunnel. "This way . . . ow!" He tripped over a B-bot.

We followed Noah to the next ladder and then through more twisting service tunnels. After we descended yet another ladder, Noah stopped to get his bearings. He consulted his app again.

"We're almost there," he announced.

After two more turns, Noah stopped and pointed to the robot opening in front of him. "If I'm right, this should be near the back of the cafeteria."

I scanned the wall and quickly found the door. I hit the push bar and swung it open. Noah was right, we were at the back of the cafeteria, near the vending machines.

"Eep!" cried a startled Maggie Ortiz, her dollar nearly falling from her outstretched hand.

"Hi," I said, giving her a small wave.

She stared blankly as the rest of us filed into the cafeteria. Other than Maggie, no one else noticed our arrival. Everyone was just as we saw them on the monitors, sitting at tables, milling around, and just generally looking bored. What a fun field trip this had turned out to be.

"Okay, who do we report this to?" asked Sam.

"I don't know," I replied. "Someone in security? Or that guy my dad left in charge, Mr. Brodigan?"

"What if one of them is in on it?" asked Noah.

Rowan pushed past me. "I'm going to go find my dad."

"Wait," I said, but it was too late. He disappeared into the crowd of kids.

"You know he's our only eyewitness, right?" asked Noah.

I nodded. "I'll find him. But everyone else split up, okay?" I asked. "We should all report it to someone different, just in case."

"Got it," said Sam.

"Okay," said Amy.

"On it," said Noah.

We separated and I made my way through the crowded cafeteria. It wasn't long before I spotted Rowan, his eyes scanning the room. I caught his eye and waved him over.

"I can't find my dad," he said.

"Maybe he was in another part of the building when everything locked down, like we were," I suggested. "But I'll help you look. Just stick with me for now."

Rowan moved away but I kept an eye him while I scanned the group for his dad. But then I spotted Mr. Brodigan. "Mr. Brodigan!" I called, waving him over.

He strode over. "How can I help you, Mr. . . ." He snapped his fingers. "T! That's right. Mr. T." He laughed and then scowled. "I pity the fool who puts me in quarantine!"

I stared at him blankly for a second before ignoring whatever reference he was trying to make. I'm telling you—adults can be so weird. "There's been a security breach," I said. "In the server room."

Mr. Brodigan's brow furrowed. "What? How would you know that?"

"Because I have a witness," I said. I turned and spotted Rowan. "Rowan! Come here for a minute."

Rowan turned to face me and gasped when he saw Mr. Brodigan. His wide eyes filled with fear.

Rowan recognized him.

13

The Apprehension Contention

ROWAN SPUN AROUND AND TOOK OFF. HE ZIG-zagged into the nearby crowd.

"Rowan!" I shouted.

I turned to chase after him but Mr. Brodigan caught my arm. "Listen, kid. I don't know what that boy told you, but it sounds as if someone has an overly active imagination."

I glared at him. "I don't think so."

"Hey, who would believe the crazy stories of some little kid?" Mr. Brodigan scoffed.

"I believe him," I said.

Mr. Brodigan shook my arm. "And who's going to believe you?"

"May I have your attention, please?" asked the automated female PA voice from before. "Quarantine is now lifted. Quarantine is now lifted."

The cafeteria was filled with applause and cheers.

The doors flew open and my father marched in. He glanced around. "*What* is going on here?"

Mr. Brodigan kept his tight grip as he dragged me over to my father. "Thank goodness you're here, boss," he said. "I think a quarantine drill was wrongly scheduled and the lock-in became a, well . . . a lockdown." He laughed nervously.

"So that's why I was locked out of my own building," my dad said. Then he crossed his arms and nodded down at me. "And what's this about?"

Mr. Brodigan jumped in before I could answer. "Oh, nothing to concern yourself with, sir." He rolled his eyes and gave another nervous laugh. "A couple of the kids came up with this wild conspiracy theory about the quarantine." He shook his head. "Crazy stuff."

I smiled up at Mr. Brodigan. "You asked who would believe me?" I nodded up at my father. "My dad would."

"Your . . . what?" Realization flickered in Mr. Brodigan's wide eyes. He gasped and released me as if my arm were red-hot.

A security guard emerged from the crowd. Amy marched right behind him. "Mr. Swift, sir? I think you ought to hear this."

Sam and Noah arrived with security guards of their own.

Mr. Brodigan eyed me nervously as I explained how we were all trapped outside of the cafeteria during the lockdown. I told him how we found the B-bot tunnels, discovered that the security cameras had been bypassed, and saw what the robots were dumping down the trash chutes.

Amy dug out the recovered hard drive and handed it to my father. He turned it over in his hands. "This is one of the company backup drives," he explained. "It might've been days before we discovered they were missing."

I pointed to Mr. Brodigan. "And he would've been long gone by then."

Noah's eyes widened. "Oh man. It was this guy?"

"No, it couldn't have been me," said Mr. Brodigan.

"I've been locked up here with everyone else." He turned to me. "You found me here, remember?" he pleaded. "Before the quarantine was lifted."

"Except he was able to bypass the lockdown to sneak out," Sam explained. "Wouldn't be too hard to sneak back in."

"He bypassed the security cameras and had access to the elevator, too," Noah added. "If you play back the video, Mr. Swift, I bet you'll find a convenient glitch leading from here all the way to the server room."

All eyes were on Mr. Brodigan. He looked around, mouth agape. "Uh—! I mean, come on. All this because one little kid says he saw me?"

"You *know* he saw you," I said. "Because you tried to pull him back into the server room with you."

"Pull him . . . what? This is crazy!" Mr. Brodigan threw up his hands and glanced around. "Where is this kid, huh?"

That was a good question. I scanned the cafeteria but there was no sign of Rowan. Our star witness had vanished. Did Mr. Brodigan have an accomplice after all? Did that accomplice now have Rowan because he could identify Mr. Brodigan? Was Mr. Kavner actually in on it?

And keeping his son from saying anything? My chest felt heavy, as if all of this would have been for—

No, wait! I spotted him. Rowan and his father walked into the cafeteria and strolled up to us.

"You know, the wind tunnel sounds like a cool place to be trapped for a couple of hours," said Mr. Kavner. "But let me tell you, it gets boring real quick." He smiled at everyone. "Rowan tells me you had quite an adventure."

Mr. Brodigan leaned forward. "Ah, there he is," the man said in a syrupy tone.

Rowan pushed in against his father.

"That wasn't me you saw, was it, kiddo?" Mr. Brodigan's eyes narrowed. "I mean, to a kid your age, all grown-ups look alike, right?"

Rowan didn't tremble this time. Instead, he glared back at Mr. Brodigan and reached into his T-shirt pocket.

"What's that?" asked Mr. Brodigan. "Whatcha got there, sport?"

Rowan pulled out the tiny body cam and handed it to his dad.

"Just my personal body cam," said Mr. Kavner. "Very cool device. Records hours and hours of video."

"And . . . that's been on the whole time, huh?" asked Mr. Brodigan.

Rowan tightened his lips and nodded.

My dad turned to one of the security guards. "Hank, please detain Mr. Brodigan and call the police."

Mr. Brodigan didn't have anything else to say as two guards escorted him out of the cafeteria.

My dad addressed the remaining guard. "And, Wayne, take the police to the basement when they get here. It sounds as if they'll find plenty of evidence in the company trash receptacles."

"Don't forget this," Mr. Kavner said as he handed my dad the body cam. "But I'll need that back for my research." He gave a wide grin. "I have a new angle for my story: Junior reporter stops corporate espionage!"

Finally, I wasn't the focus of the story anymore. I exhaled as a wave of relief crashed over me.

"Uh, remember," said Noah. "Tom helped, too."

I glared at him. "Dude!"

"We all did," Rowan added, smiling up at us.

After the security guards were gone, my dad crossed his arms and cocked his head. "So, tell me if

I have this right," he said. "None of you were locked in with the others *and* were able to help catch the bad guy because . . . you're essentially workaholics?"

Sam cringed. "Well, it sounds kinda bad when you put it like that."

Amy nodded. "No, that's about right."

"Well, *they* were working," I said, putting a hand on Rowan's shoulder. "I was just hanging out with a friend."

Rowan grinned up at me.

"Ah," my dad said, raising one eyebrow. "So, I guess you're a Formidable Fivesome now."

"Still good alliteration," Sam pointed out.

"Oh yeah," I agreed. "I think Rowan will make an excellent Swift Academy student."

Luckily, the quarantine didn't put a damper on the events of the evening. Everyone went back to his or her projects while my friends and I gave statements to the police. After that, my dad and I showed Rowan and Mr. Kavner the rest of the facility—using the regular hallways this time. When we were finished, everyone met up with Sam at the test track.

Once the air-conditioning vent was closed and the

mats were returned to the wall, Sam had the chance to make her fastest run yet: 46.3 kph. I also got the chance to redeem myself on her new skates.

After I was strapped head-to-toe with safety gear, I sat and put on the skates.

"He's got this," my dad said confidently. "We Rollerblade all the time."

Yeah, no pressure, I thought. *Thanks, Dad.*

When I was all set, Sam and Noah each took one of my arms and helped me to my feet. I wobbled a bit at first, but then felt the gyroscopes do their thing. I quickly leveled out.

"You can do this, dude," said Noah.

"Easy-peasy," Sam agreed.

Rowan cupped his hands around his mouth. "Remember, don't fight it!" he yelled from the sidelines.

"What, you're an expert now?" Mr. Kavner asked him.

"Oh yeah," Amy replied. She sat on the ground next to Otis. "He's a natural."

I swayed just once more as I rolled down the track. I kicked out ever so slightly with my right foot to gain speed, and it worked! I didn't fall down. I repeated the motion with my left foot and everything was fine. Feeling better, I leaned forward to go faster.

"Woo-hoo!" Sam yelled.

"You got it now!" shouted Noah.

My confidence grew along with my speed. I was doing it! No invention was going to get the better of me. I felt as if I could conquer anything.

As I came up to the curve, I began to lean into it. The trouble was, I leaned too much. My right foot moved too far out and the skates automatically compensated. Even though I knew it was coming, the movement still surprised me. I naturally fought it before I realized what I was doing. I tried to relax and go with the flow as I'd been told.

By then it was too late.

The skates went out from under me and I landed, once again, on the only part of my body that wasn't covered in safety gear.

"Oh!" Noah shouted. "Wipeout!"

I laughed and rubbed my sore backside. Man, I missed that spongy track at the school.

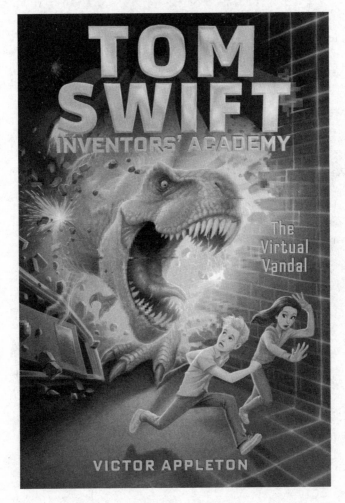

The Simulation
Demonstration

THE THREE OF US SLOWLY MADE OUR WAY UP THE
dark steps. I led the way, followed by my friends Amy
Hsu and Samantha Watson. As we stepped out onto
the third floor, I aimed my flashlight into the empty
corridor. I could feel my heart beating faster with
anticipation.

"This is really creepy," Amy whispered. "Cool, but
creepy."

"Why are you whispering?" Sam asked. "We're the
only ones here."

"Because we're creeping around the school at night,"

Amy replied. "Even if it's not really . . ." She trailed off as she whipped her flashlight back down the stairs. Sam and I froze, listening.

Then Amy relaxed, and we continued down the hall. "Besides—" She went back to a whisper. "Noah might be spying on us."

"Of course he's spying on us," I said with a chuckle. "He worked too hard on this *not* to spy on us." I glanced around. "Isn't that right, dude?"

There was no reply.

"That would've been too easy, Swift," Sam said as she led the way down the dark corridor.

Noah Newton, my best friend, had created a special scavenger hunt for us. And the setting for this hunt? Our school, the Swift Academy of Science and Technology. At night, of course.

If the name of our school sounds familiar, it's because it was named after my father, Tom Swift Sr. He founded the academy with profits from his company, Swift Enterprises. If you think it would be cool to have all these places with your last name on them, you'd be wrong. Honestly, it just means I have to work harder to be a regular student like everyone else.

A flash of light burst through a nearby window. Soon after, the walls seemed to rattle with the deep boom of thunder.

"The thunderstorm is a nice touch," I said to Noah, wherever he was. He still didn't reply.

Sam stopped moving forward. "What was the clue again?"

Amy responded automatically. Having a photographic memory, she had already memorized it when she had first read it. "'Once on the third floor, don't be afraid of the dark,'" she replied. "'Find not the king of the jungle, but the king of the park.'"

"Who's the king of the park?" I asked.

"A lion is supposed to be the king of the jungle," Sam replied. "Even though they technically don't live in jungles."

"What about in Mrs. Livingston's classroom?" asked Amy. "She has a lion poster in there."

"It's worth a shot," I said.

We glided down the hallway toward our biology classroom. I swung open the door and reached for the light switch. I heard the switch click but the overhead lights didn't come on. The only light came through the windows and barely illuminated the room.

The three of us poured in and made our way to the wall behind Mrs. Livingston's desk. Hung there was a motivational poster about courage, sporting a large lion with a thick, shaggy mane. I'm not sure if Mrs. Livingston had it up there to remind us to be courageous and ask questions, or because of her notoriously difficult exams.

"Wait a minute," said Sam. She stopped moving. "The clue said *not* the king of the jungle."

"That's right," I agreed, glancing around. "But who would be king of the park?"

Amy pointed to a poster on the other side of the classroom. "What about that one?"

I turned and squinted across the room. I had completely forgotten that Mrs. Livingston also had a tyrannosaurus rex poster at the back of the classroom. It wasn't a motivational poster or anything; it was just part of a cool dinosaur display she had created. The exhibition also included a fossilized megalodon tooth, the fossilized femur of an Edmontosaurus, and a cast Mrs. Livingston made of a real dinosaur footprint (a small theropod of some kind).

"King of the park," Sam said, excitement rising in her voice. "Like Jurassic Park."

"Even though the T. rex really lived during the Cretaceous period," Amy added.

"Yeah, but *Cretaceous Park* doesn't have the same ring to it," I said as I made my way toward the poster.

We all gathered around it. On it, a huge T. rex stood in the clearing of a prehistoric forest. It grinned at us, its mouth full of jagged teeth.

"The poster is exactly the same," Amy observed. "Noah didn't add anything to it."

"Maybe he hid something behind it," Sam suggested. She reached out and grabbed the bottom left corner of the poster. But when she lifted up the flap, the corner jerked itself away from her and snapped back to the wall.

"What the . . . ," Sam began.

Then the entire poster began to expand. We stood back as the bottom of the picture slid down the wall and onto the baseboards. The top of the poster stretched up toward the ceiling as the entire thing grew. Soon, the image of the terrifying dinosaur covered the whole wall.

"What's going on?" asked Amy.

The dinosaur was now life-size. My heart raced as it glared down at us. Then, as if it couldn't get any stranger than that, the T. rex moved. Just a blink of an eye at first, and then one of its two-clawed hands closed.

"Did you just see that?!" Sam asked in an entire octave above her normal speaking voice.

Before anyone could answer, one of the dinosaur's huge feet stepped *out* of the poster. It scattered the fossil display and crashed down on a nearby desk. We moved back as the desk shattered.

Above us, the T. rex *leaned out* of the poster! Its long snout stretched and contorted as 2-D slowly became 3-D. As it loomed over us, it cocked its head and examined us with one large eye. Its mouth opened wider, long tendrils of saliva dripping down from above.

"Run!" I shouted.

The three of us bolted toward the door as the T. rex roared. I chanced a glance back to see the full-size tyrannosaurus rex on our tails, crashing through desks as it chased after us.

My heart raced faster as we ran out of the classroom and headed toward the closest stairwell. Amy and Sam shot past me as I checked behind us. There was no way that huge dinosaur would fit through the classroom door. . . .

Boy, was I wrong. The T. rex burst through the wall. Shattered cinderblocks and splintered wood ricocheted down the empty corridor as the creature skidded to a stop in the middle of the hallway. It sniffed and whipped its head in our direction. My blood turned to ice.

I flew down the stairs and caught up to my friends as they entered the first floor. I could hear the dinosaur barreling down the stairwell behind us. There probably wouldn't be any steps left by the time it reached the bottom.

"Unbelievable," Sam said as she glanced back.

We darted down the main corridor, toward the gym.

"What's that?" Amy asked, pointing ahead.

There was a small wooden box on the floor ahead of us. It sat conspicuously in the middle of the hallway, right in front of the open gym doors. We came to a stop next to it and I lifted the lid. Several long red cylinders lined the box.

"Is that dynamite?" Amy asked.

"We're supposed to stop a dinosaur with dynamite?" asked Sam.

As if on cue, the huge T. rex crashed to the bottom of the stairwell. Dust and debris filled the air as the dinosaur lumbered through the entryway and stomped into the first-floor hallway. It paused to give another bone-chilling roar before moving in our direction.

I pulled out one of the sticks of dynamite and turned it over in my hands.

"It doesn't have a fuse," I said disarmingly.

"Does anyone have matches or a lighter?" asked Sam. "How could we light it even if it did have a fuse?"

The T. rex roared again as it ran closer.

"W-w—what do we do?" stammered Amy.

"Oh man," said a familiar voice. "You guys are *so* going to get eaten."

Suddenly, as if by magic, Noah appeared between us and the charging dinosaur. He reached into the wooden box and pulled out a stick of dynamite. Noah removed a clear cap off one end of the stick and brought it toward the other end, and then I realized that it wasn't dynamite at all. With a quick motion, he scraped them against each other, like striking a match. The road flare ignited with a hissing, sparking red light.

"Check it out," Noah said as he turned to face the charging beast.

The T. rex slid to a stop in front of the flare. Its giant head stretched forward and tracked the bright light as

Noah moved it from right to left, and then left to right. Then Noah tossed the flare through the open gym doors. The dinosaur took off after it, twisting the metal doorjamb as it squeezed through the entryway. We watched as it disappeared into the dark gym.

"Aw, man," Sam said. "We should've guessed that one."

"I put a hint in the clue and everything," Noah said.

"The same way Dr. Grant tried to distract the T. rex in *Jurassic Park*," Amy added.

"Except it worked when I did it," said Noah.

"Dude," I said, turning to my best friend. "That was awesome!" I extended a fist toward him.

Noah reached out and our fists simply passed through each other.

Amy giggled.

Noah sighed. "Yeah, I never could get that to actually work in here."

"So . . . that's it?" asked Sam. She peered into the dark gym. "The T. rex isn't coming back?"

"No, this is where his program ends," replied Noah. "And he'll completely reset in a minute or so. I was thinking about making him play basketball when he's in the gym. But I ran out of time."

"That would've been funny," Amy said. "With those little arms."

"I know, right?" asked Noah. "I spent way too much time on him already, though."

"I can tell," I said. "Amazing detail."

"Thanks," Noah said. His avatar gave a polite bow.

Sam, Amy, and I just had the honor of being the first to test Noah's new virtual reality program. That's right—my best bud was a brilliant programmer. And for the past several months, he had been using every bit of his free time to create a virtual Swift Academy. Of course, he didn't have time to reproduce *every* classroom, but what he did create looked impressively accurate, right down to the smallest detail.

Noah even did a great job on our four avatars. Each of our characters looked lifelike—it seemed as if we were actually in the school's first-floor hallway when, in actuality, we were each in our own homes.

Noah created a system where we could put our phones in a special visor. Then we could connect to the program through Wi-Fi or our cell service. The program itself was on the school servers so we could log on and view the virtual world through our phones no matter where we were. Add a special controller for each hand and we could move our hands and pick up virtual items in his virtual school.

"You guys did great until the end there," Noah said.

"So you *were* spying on us," said Amy. "I knew it."

"Of course," Noah said. "I had to see how you would react."

"How did you do it?" Sam asked.

"The easiest way I could think of," Noah replied. His avatar's left hand reached over and touched his right hand, which probably meant that Noah was pushing a button on the controller in real life. Then Noah disappeared.

"Cool," said Amy.

"I can make my character invisible and intangible," Noah's disembodied voice explained. "But I can still pick stuff up." A road flare rose from the wooden box and seemed to float around by itself.

"Good way to cheat at hide-and-seek," Sam said. "What button makes you invisible?"

"Sorry," Noah said as he reappeared. "Only the creator has that power."

Sam's avatar shook her head. "Figures."

Amy's avatar looked to the left. "I have to go," she said. "My mother's calling me for dinner."

"I'd better be going too," Sam added. "Thanks for letting us try your program."

"Yes, thank you," Amy agreed. "It's really cool."

"I'm glad you liked it," Noah replied. His program wasn't sophisticated enough to relay facial expressions, but I could tell from the sound of his voice that he was grinning from ear to ear.

I raised my hand and my avatar gave them a wave. "See you tomorrow."

The girls waved back before their avatars faded to nothing.

"So you're going to turn it in to Mr. Varma tomorrow?" I asked Noah.

"Yeah," he replied. "Then I'm going to open-source it for everyone."

"Really?" I asked. "So anyone can change any part of it?"

"Just about," he replied. "They'll be able to customize their avatars, add characters, change the different environments, create side missions ..."

"Wow," I said. "Do you have any idea what you'll be unleashing?"

Noah's avatar nodded. "I can't wait to see what people come up with. But don't worry. We'll still have the basement to ourselves. That's unchangeable."

"Cool," I said.

When Noah created the game, he had our four avatars spawn in the basement. And only the four of us had access to that part of the school. We even used the access code we already had memorized thanks to a previous . . . mishap involving drones and the FBI.

See? Things get weird in the real Swift Academy, not just the virtual one.

"And . . ." Noah said, his avatar raising both hands. "Now I'll finally be able to pull my weight with *our* two projects."

"Don't worry, I'll put you to work tomorrow," I said. "But first I have a question. . . . Will the T. rex chase you if you remain completely still, like in the movies?"

Noah's avatar raised his hands in an exaggerated shrug. "I guess you'll have to try and see."

"Let's do it!" I said, and I moved my avatar down the hall. Noah and I ran up the stairs to give the T. rex another try.